RV, the Racer Aardvark

A Whacked Out World Where the Races are WARPED

Eccentric Racing Network

Written and Illustrated

BY

L. M. RUTTKAY

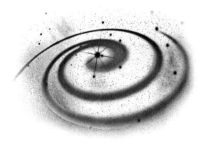

For information regarding permission, write to:
Eccentric Racing Network
P.O. Box 2847 San Marcos, CA 92709

10 9 8 7 6 5 4 3 2 1

ISBN: 978-0-9819491-3-0
Library of Congress control number: TX0001356387
Printed and bound in the U.S.A.

Cover design by L. M. Ruttkay
Interior Design & Typesetting by Jill Ronsley, suneditwrite.com

To Justin Ruttkay,
Broc Costa and Kelly Costa Gravitt

A Special "Thank you" to Mike Hill
and the Alien Workshop

CONTENTS

CHAPTER ONE

THE BEGINNING

Once upon a time on the planet Zein, thousands of light years from Earth, a rare phenomenon occurred: the least likely inhabitant became an unexpected legend.

On Zein, you will find that the laws of nature are highly unpredictable, and the life forms tend to be strange in comparison with those on Earth. The ardvercurean, for example, is very similar to the human being. It can reason and make moral decisions, and yet this species has a curiously tubular snout, large ears, and even a tail. The slang term, aardvark, is often used for this creature because of its distinct anatomical features.

This is the story of one very ordinary blue Zeinian aardvark. His name was RV, and he might never have become exceptional if it hadn't been for the defect at his birth. RV was born without feet.

It looked as though his quality of life would surely be diminished; however, the painful providence would shape his future in a way that no one ever could have expected.

RV was very little when his father made a wheel for him to use in place of feet. The apparatus was fixed on an axle between his shortened lower limbs and fastened with a bolt on each side. At first, the young aardvark found it difficult to balance on one wheel, and he worked very hard just to get around. He had so many setbacks that he often wanted to give up, and it seemed doubtful that he would ever become fully independent.

As time went on, the youngster became captivated by the speed and agility of race vehicles. He began to study how their wheels moved and handled turns. RV thought in his heart, *I could do that.* Soon he fell in love with every sport that required wheels—but he wanted to be a racer most of all.

Cruel bystanders would laugh at the aardvark with the homemade wheel. They teased and called him names, but RV paid little attention. The aspiring athlete continued to push himself until he could maneuver so well on one wheel that he became incredibly fast.

By the time he was nineteen years old, RV was a first class unicycle racer. He became known as "RV, the Racer Aardvark." The wheel had become so much a part of him that no one could imagine him, or would even want to imagine him, without it.

"It's a race!" RV would shout as he took off speeding, but the only thing the eye could ever see was a *blur of blue* whizzing past. It was a *blur of blue* that lifted your spirits and reminded you that anything was possible.

One day, RV was training on a field near the Major Harbor when his friend, Fast Earnie, showed up and challenged him to a race. RV liked to race just for the fun of it, and he loved to race with his friends. The two spent hours in their own personal practice area.

The track, as they liked to call it, was set in a coastal field amid anderlies, orchanvillies, and paramid flowers. The place absolutely shimmered with radiant light from the suns. (I say suns, because Zein has three suns and four moons.) The entire place was awe-inspiring with all seven globes in full view. The aqua blue ocean in the distance further enhanced their splendor. It was truly magnificent!

Suddenly the *blur of blue* whizzed past. Fast Earnie held up his stopwatch.

"Yes! You beat your time. This has to be a Zeinian record. I don't think anyone's ever done this before!"

"That was definitely fun," said RV as he slapped Fast Earnie a high five.

Fast Earnie was RV's most trusted and loyal friend. He was a mobilot. The best way to describe a mobilot is to imagine a creature that is part man, part robot, and part vehicle. Whenever Fast Earnie wore his race helmet, he was able to morph from a man into a vehicle, and back again, if he wanted to do so. He had a silver-blue hue with red trim, and he was a first-class fast track racer. Since the two friends raced in different divisions, they were able to help each other, contributing greatly to their success.

"Hey, RV! I need to head out and get back to my sweetie-pie," said his pal.

Fast Earnie had recently married the beautiful Madame Insane, and as far as RV could tell, it was true love. He was really happy for his friend. These two guys were such ardent athletes, and it was surprising to discover that they were just as passionate about finding the right girl to marry. Perhaps that heartfelt desire had deepened their friendship. The idea of holding out "for the right one" motivated both of them.

RV took a deep breath and watched Fast Earnie drive off. He laughed to himself when he noticed how out of place their wheel-worn track looked in the middle of the Zeinian field of dreams. Then his thoughts drifted, and he decided to go to the DLG Café in town.

RV was a romantic. There was only one thing that he loved more than racing, and that was Deluxe—sweet, fine Deluxe. She worked as a waitress at the DLG Café while studying to become a fine artist.

Deluxe was also a Zeinian aardvark. However, she was not blue, and like most aardvarks on the planet, she had two feet. RV liked her so much. She could talk about both simple and deep things, and what she said was always interesting. As far as he could tell, Deluxe only liked him as a friend. That was all right; having her for a friend was better than not having her in his life at all.

RV approached the DLG Café and saw an open table in the patio section. He rolled up to it and noticed a copy of the *Major Times* newspaper lying on top. The newspaper headline read, MAJOR RACES COMING SOON: Amazing New Unicycle Division. He laid the paper aside, laughed to himself, and thought, *It seems like someone really wants me to race in that new unicycle division. I keep getting letters and calls, and lately, I keep finding hints everywhere I go. I wonder who put this paper here.*

Deluxe was serving customers at another table when she caught his eye. RV was amused and thought, *Look at that! She is so cute. I'll bet she's cheering up those folks at that table. She's always doing stuff like that. I think she has to be the most thoughtful ... Oh, here she comes!*

Deluxe walked up to RV's table. He noticed that she was wearing a purple halter-top with a green emchial gem in the center strap. She wore her little DLG apron over her blue canaveras shorts. She looked at him with brilliant blue eyes and smiled.

"I can't imagine that you would want caffeine—as if you needed any more energy!" said Deluxe.

"No, no. I thought you were getting off work now," said RV. "Fast Earnie and I just ripped on our new practice field.

You have to come out and see it, Deluxe. It's right smack in the middle of wild orchanvillies … so pretty. I know how much you love orchanvillies."

RV beamed with enthusiasm. He talked so quickly that it seemed he hardly took a breath. He made Deluxe smile.

"Okay, cool! Let's do it. I would like to see that. I have plenty of time before I have to be at my class this afternoon," she said. And she set her tray on an empty table nearby.

Deluxe had responded so favorably to his invitation that he wanted to show off in front of her. He held up a large gold coin.

"Hey, hang on!" he said. "I've got to give you a tip. Just keep your eyes on this coin, okay?"

"Okay," said Deluxe. She knew he wanted to show her a trick, so she decided to challenge him. "Let's see what you can do."

RV sat down and began his performance with confidence.

"Now, I am going to make this coin go right through this table. Would you please hand me an empty glass?"

"There you go," said Deluxe as she handed him a glass from her tray.

RV winked at her.

"We'll just cover the glass with this napkin … like so."

He held the covered glass over the coin with one hand and waved his other hand over the glass as if to make the coin disappear. At a nearby table, a humatozoid mommy held her fourteen-month-old baby, unaware that while her little one was sucking on his pacifier, he was intently watching RV's every move.

Deluxe folded her arms and egged RV on.

"Now what?" she said.

RV carefully lifted the covered glass.

"WALLAH!" he said.

This would have been very impressive except that the coin was still on the table. Deluxe looked perplexed.

"Are you sure you know how to do this?" she said.

At first she had hoped RV's trick would impress her, but now she was embarrassed for him. She considered that perhaps he might not be skilled at doing tricks, after all. However, the aardvark performer was undeterred.

"Hmm," RV said as he scratched his head. "Let's try that again." After he went through all the same maneuvers, he picked up the covered glass and said, "WALLAH!"

Once again, the coin had not disappeared.

"I don't know, RV. This trick isn't going so hot," said Deluxe.

RV placed a covered glass over the coin again.

"Okay, okay. One more time," he said. "You know, since the coin isn't disappearing, maybe let's just …"

He never finished his sentence. He smacked his hand down hard on the glass—which then disappeared into the table!

"Like I was saying—let's just make the glass disappear too!"

The baby's pacifier dropped out of his mouth. He continued to make puckering sounds as he stared at the table with big round eyes. RV picked up the napkin to show that the coin and the glass had both disappeared. Then he pulled the coin out from under the table and handed it to Deluxe.

"How did you do that?" said Deluxe. She was amazed. She looked more closely at the coin and realized what kind of souvenir he had just given her. "Hey! Where did you get this? This is a rare coin!"

"That's your tip. You're an awesome waitress," said RV.

"But where did the glass go?" said Deluxe.

"Look over there." RV pointed to the tray where the glass was now sitting. Then he playfully hugged her and said, "Come on, let's go. I want to show you the track."

As they left the café, RV looked back and waved bye-bye to the little guy.

CHAPTER TWO

ORCHANVILLY FIELDS FOREVER

RV and Deluxe approached the edge of a steep cliff that gave them an excellent view of the orchanvilly fields. The scenery below was picturesque: green pastures dotted with flowers, set against a backdrop of white sandy dunes that stretched to the beach. It was a glorious sight indeed! However, RV sensed that Deluxe was nervous. He held her hand as they neared the edge. The sheer height of the cliffs was intimidating and would make almost anyone anxious.

RV was not afraid at all, which was remarkable, considering that he had a wheel beneath him. He was a strong athlete. It had taken great self-control and patience to learn to function with a wheel instead of feet. He had become compassionate towards others because of this and was well aware of Deluxe's apprehension

The twisted, bizarre features of the cliffs were impressive. In certain places, the crags and protrusions on the surface of the sediment appeared to have been created by some malevolent force of nature; in others, the rock formations were delightful and almost whimsical. Most of the cliff was peculiarly formed, but a few spots provided a convenient passageway down to the beach. RV had discovered a perfect path that connected steps and caves, slides and walkways.

RV led Deluxe down the footpath, holding her hand and sharing amusing stories to distract her from the challenge of getting down to the beach. He told her about the famous tourist attraction to the north called the Braggadocio Hole. Deluxe peered in the distance and saw visitors standing around the geyser, watching its spray shoot high in the air. Then RV pointed to Old Castle Island out in the ocean. The Old Castle was difficult to see, but the island was fascinating. It had become the subject of much folklore since it had been vacant for nearly a century.

RV found out what really sparked Deluxe's interest when he mentioned Fast Earnie.

"Wait until you see the field that Fast Earnie and I turned into a practice track," said RV, watching Deluxe concentrate on every step. "He had to leave early to get back home to his wife. I remember when those two first met."

"Oh yeah, Madame Insane! He met her at the DLG while I was working. He's crazy about her. That man certainly loves his wife," said Deluxe.

RV was taken aback. He was surprised by her eager response, and he took a deep gulp when she spoke so openly about romance.

"Really?" he replied. He was unable to think of anything better to say.

Deluxe innocently nodded. "Oh, yes," she said. "You wouldn't believe it. Every time Fast Earnie meets someone new and introduces Madame Insane, he tells the whole story of how they met at the DLG. I can't believe how many times I've heard that story. Customers ask me all the time if Fast Earnie really met his wife where I work."

She was happily absorbed in conversation. RV was pleased that it kept her calm; at the same time, he couldn't help but be in awe of her. Didn't she know how much he liked her? This spirited recollection of Fast Earnie and Madame Insane's relationship had caught him off guard. He had to admit that he was learning more about Madame Insane from Deluxe than he had ever learned from Fast Earnie.

Madame Insane was beautiful, and everyone knew it. What RV didn't know was why she was called "Insane." Her parents hadn't given her that name. One would think that being called "Insane" would be an insult, but in her case, it meant something too wonderful for words to describe.

Madame Insane exuded mystery that surpassed all the mysteries of womankind. She was a stunning combination of warmth, humor, and intrigue. On Zein, she would be classified as an extremely lovely humatazoid—a glamorous character with her long, flowing red hair, twinkling blue eyes, and crooked, oversized smile. She also had power—power she used wisely.

Deluxe giggled as RV helped her down the last step where the track was located. She was still engrossed in conversation when she looked up and saw the delightful view of the orchanvillies surrounding them.

"Ah!" Deluxe sighed, reached down, and delicately picked one of the blossoms. "Oh RV, this is beautiful!"

Her response to her favorite flower made him smile.

"Did you know that the orchanvilly is the only flower on the planet that stays in bloom its entire lifetime?" RV said, hoping to impress her. "The flower closes every night, and the old bloom transforms into a new one that appears in the morning. It's miraculous."

"You know, I remember reading a poem about orchanvillies by Judd Magen," Deluxe said dreamily. "Now that you've told me how these flowers appear to live forever, his poem makes so much more sense. He compared the orchanvilly to undying love. He wrote, 'What a man desires is undying love.'"

Well, that did it! *Undying love?* RV had always enjoyed the way Deluxe viewed life through art and poetry; it was one of the things he liked about her. But come on! Undying love? What was a guy supposed to think? He started to perspire. All this love talk really made him nervous, and he wasn't used to being nervous.

He began to stutter and searched for a way to feel comfortable again.

"O-o-o-kay … Okay. That, that's amazing … yeah, that's amazing," he said as he caught his breath. He took the flower from Deluxe's hand and changed the direction of the conversation. "Okay. Let's put this in your hair. I want you to prepare because I am going to take you on a test drive around this track."

He helped her onto his back, and his confidence returned as he focused on the athletic playtime ahead. "Trust me now. This will be sort of like a piggyback ride, but on an aardvark."

RV rode around the track with speed and grace, carrying Deluxe piggyback-style just as he had promised. The landscape was beautiful, with green ground cover, orchanvillies, and paramid flowers. In the distance, giant waves rolled and crashed in the aqua blue ocean.

The wind blew through Deluxe's hair, and the sunlight warmed her face. She closed her eyes as if to capture this thrilling moment of unique fun forever in her memory. When she opened them again, the field had become animated. She saw orchanvillies everywhere, swaying in the breeze. They took flight, swarmed all around, and gracefully constructed an arch through which she and RV traveled.

Then a pelican-like bird called a mygratia flew by their side. Deluxe patted RV on the shoulder to get his attention and pointed at it. These birds rarely came so close. She could have reached out and touched its wing, except that they were moving too quickly.

The mygratia continued along for a while, and then it winked at them. RV and Deluxe were delighted—until the creature suddenly disintegrated into crystalline sparkles before their eyes. They were baffled! Was this some sort of trick?

Deluxe playfully put her hands over RV's eyes and quickly released them. This, of course, caused his vision to go black for an instant. Normally, he wouldn't like that kind of gesture, but she was having so much fun, and he saw no harm in humoring her.

RV teased her in return. When she tried to cover his eyes again, he pulled back his arms and flipped her high in the sky. Talk about being taken by surprise! Deluxe didn't know what had hit her. She was in the air before there was any time to be afraid. He caught her safely over his head and held her there as they continued to travel at a great speed. It was remarkable how startled, yet safe, she felt at the same time. Boldly, she stretched her arms out at her sides like wings. She was fearless.

The anderlies, or butterfly-like creatures, swirled around them. Suddenly a tree disintegrated before them, just as the mygratia had done; and yet another tree evaporated into thin air. Some sort of wizardry of disappearing creation had intruded upon this wonderfully alive field.

RV and Deluxe were too busy having fun to pay much attention to it. He flipped her up again. This time he caught her in his arms and twirled and twirled and twirled her.

CHAPTER THREE

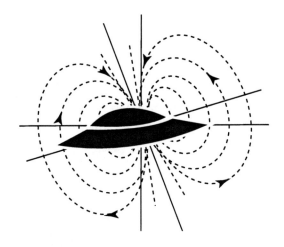

UNIDENTIFIED
FLYING OBJECT

RV was in seventh heaven as he held Deluxe in his arms. They stared up at the sky and laughed. The sky appeared to move right along with them and actually seemed to be spinning. (That would be impossible, though, wouldn't it? I mean, the sky doesn't twirl or move along with anyone—although even I have to admit, sometimes it does seem like it moves. But trust me, even on Zein, it just doesn't work that way. Anyway, let's continue.)

Far above the clouds, something disturbing was traveling along with them. RV and Deluxe were unaware that a suspicious spacecraft hovered over them, watching their every move. It had stopped above the orchanvilly fields around the time they finished their hike down the side of the cliff.

The uneven vibration of sound that characterized a flying saucer could be heard. Closer to its force field, the *whoosh-hum, whoosh-hum* pattern became more distinct.

A silvery white sphere rotated in place in the sky. The technical design details of the vehicle were simple, yet refined. The upper portion was shaped like a globe cut off at the top, and the smooth silver bottom and lower edges gradually blended into a metallic trim of yellow, green, and blue. The upper dome was made of highly reflective one-way glass. This camouflaged the flying saucer and allowed it to blend into the sky, making it easy for the pilots to spy on others.

"Aw, isn't that sweet?" said the spacecraft commander.

It was the sinister Major Tomm, mocking RV and Deluxe. The Major was envious of the racer aardvark, and he insisted on ridiculing him even from afar.

"It's RV and Deluxe frolicking in the field," he continued.

Major Tomm's assistant, E-racer, was watching RV and Deluxe ride, and he really did think it was sweet.

"Yeah," E-racer said enchanted.

The Major quickly swatted him on the head, looked crossly at him, and said pointedly, "I … was … not … SERIOUS!" He looked down at RV through a portal and exclaimed, "Look at him! Look how fast he is! And he's carrying HER!"

Then for no reason at all, the Major began to march back and forth as if he was in a parade. The space inside the flying saucer was small, so in order to march back and forth, he had to turn frequently. Was this a tantrum? Was he hallucinating? E-racer thought he looked ridiculous. However, such were the weird ways of Major Tomm.

The Major was a man-droinot who looked very much like an astronaut. It is difficult to say for certain, but he may have also been part machine. He was what you would call bizarre.

Major Tomm liked to think of himself as the richest and most clever inventor of all time. While it is true that he was very rich, it is equally true that all his ingenious devices had been stolen from someone else. He cleverly embezzled the rights to inventions before the real inventors were able to patent them in their own names. Needless to say, after doing this for many years, he owned most of the businesses on Zein, and hence, the majority of the wealth.

Major Tomm was odd, wicked, and cruel beyond question. He was obsessed with what others thought of him. He wanted to be important, and the possibility of being famous was even better. Being a good person with a good reputation didn't matter to him. He didn't care if he was a good inventor, a good athlete, or a good anything. Major Tomm only cared that others should think of him as good—especially if it meant that he got all the credit. You might say that the Major just wanted to look better than everyone else.

He really didn't care about others much at all. In fact, he would say things like, "It's okay if I do this as long as it doesn't hurt anyone else." But he only said things like that for show. The truth is that whenever someone does the wrong thing, it always hurts someone else.

For Major Tomm, however, none of that mattered. The most important thing to him was getting what he wanted and making sure that others thought he was the best at everything.

Panels of colored lights blinked interchangeably in rows inside the spaceship while the Major marched back and forth on the bridge. He looked through a portal window on the console desk and watched while RV and Deluxe enjoyed their ride around the track. A colorful monitor lit up, displaying an illuminated map.

Finally, Major Tomm ended his march and yelled, "I've got to get that aardvark to race against me. I've GOT to get him to race against me!"

E-racer was the Major's short, green, and very, very bad apprentice. He also had a nervous temperament that made him stutter when he spoke. Major Tomm had done an operation years earlier and implanted one of his inventions into E-racer's body. It was a powerful piece of equipment, and E-racer had been indebted to his boss ever since.

E-racer was given a protono-coniclastic index finger that he could use to disintegrate—or *erase*—whatever he shot. He could point, shoot, and erase anything. Hence, he was given the name "E-racer." The Major utilized his services particularly at racing events in order to ensure that he always won.

Life for E-racer was all about pleasing Major Tomm. Perhaps that was why he was nervous and unsure of himself all the time.

Seeing his boss come out of his trance-like march, he said, "B-B-But M-M-Major Tomm, you're the best! You're the best!"

"Well, yes," replied the Major. He smiled in agreement as he blew on his right fist and proudly rubbed his chest with it. "Ah! That is true … so true," he continued. Suddenly, his tone of voice changed and he frowned. "But what matters is that EVERYONE BELIEVES that I am the best. Right now that aardvark is getting a little too popular."

E-racer became excited. This was his chance to prove he was a great assistant. He looked through the portal at RV and Deluxe on the orchanvilly-covered track and aimed his finger.

E-racer shot away at the scene below—shouting, "I'll shoot 'em. I'll shoot 'em!"

First a cloud disappeared. Then a mygratia disintegrated. That was really close. He almost got RV that time, but that old mygratia was in the way. He shot again and a tree disappeared.

"EEEEEE-RACER!" the apprentice shouted. "That's me."

He was all worked up. He shot one more time and another tree disappeared. The Major swatted him on the head again. E-racer was stunned by the familiar gesture of disapproval.

"Slow down there, Turbo." Disgusted, Major Tomm reprimanded his small green assistant. "Wait for my command!"

E-racer thought, *At least he's not in a trance anymore, but perhaps the trance was better than this.*

The Major said, "There will be plenty of time for *e-racing* later. First, I have to find a way to get RV, the Racer Aardvark to enter the Major Races. I want him in that Unicycle Division. Yeah, that's what I'm talking about!"

You see, one way the Major could get all the credit was to win awards. Of course, he always cheated to win. Not only did he cheat, but since he had become so rich, he also hosted the very events that gave out the awards in the first place!

One example of this was the Annual Major Races and Sporting Event, better known as the Major Races. E-racer was often required to use his *e-racer* power to disintegrate objects—particularly at this popular competition.

E-racer could not understand what was happening. He knew his boss would look good if he publicly beat RV in a race, but the aardvark was a unicycle racer. Instead of trying to figure it out, he went along with the whole thing.

"Th-th-that's in three days ... three days ... three days from now," said E-racer.

The Major tapped impatiently on the console, remembering all his attempts to persuade RV to enter the Major Races.

"I've advertised. I've sent him three letters. I've even called him on the vu-screen," said Major Tomm.

A vu-screen was a communication device on Zein that worked as a type of phone, computer, television, and aerial detector. It also had other functions. The best way to imagine a vu-screen is to think of a video screen that could be seen only when it was being used—like a video hologram. Small vu-screens could be taken anywhere. Large vu-screens were commonly known as "big screens."

Major Tomm was almost frantic. "No matter what means I've used, that aardvark has refused to race."

E-racer asked, "W-w-why? W-w-what's wrong … what's wrong with him?"

"He thinks they're rigged," said the Major.

"Oh," replied E-racer. He refrained from saying anything else.

The Major became very quiet and stared at the illuminated map on the console desk. This made his nervous associate even more apprehensive. E-racer lived to please Major Tomm, but he also lived in fear of him. The Major's behavior could be very erratic. He might appear calm, but this could last for only a moment.

Major Tomm pointed to the map and said, "E-racer, I want you to take a look at this. RV and Deluxe are here and Bombay Island is over there."

E-racer quickly shuffled close to the Major, glanced at the map, and immediately became concerned. The map named Old Castle Island as Bombay Island. What was going on?

"B-B-Bombay Island?" E-racer asked defiantly. "I thought that was O-O-Old Castle I-I-Island."

"Well, it's Bombay Island now! I gave it to Bombman," said the Major impatiently. He boasted of his power again. "I do own just about everything around here, you know."

Major Tomm proceeded to remind E-racer of all his assets. There was Major City, which was named after him.

Then there was his business, Major Income. There was Major Market, the stock market that had recently been named after him, and of course, there were all the Major Products, not to mention the Major Profits.

Major Tomm made his final point. "I can give Bombman an island if I want."

That should have ended it, but surprisingly, the little green apprentice wasn't buying it.

"B-B-Bombman has his own i-i-island?" said E-racer. "I-I-I want an island. I-I-I want an island. Why don't I have an island?"

Although these two villains shared the same characteristic of wanting their own way, E-racer always (and I might add always *unsuccessfully*) whined to get what he wanted. This only made his boss more impatient.

The Major finally said, "Let's just say that Bombman has earned it!"

He pointed again at the illuminated map. He explained, not for E-racer's sake, but for the joy of hearing himself talk about his ingenious and dastardly plan.

"Bombman is going to kidnap Deluxe. Then he's going to send a ransom note to RV that says, 'You can have the girl back … blah, blah, blah … if you bring me the Unicycle First Place Trophy from the Major Races.'"

"Humph!" said the disgruntled assistant.

Major Tomm was mentally somewhere else again. He pretended that the crowds were cheering for him.

"Yes!" he said as if he was congratulating himself. "RV will enter the Major Races. You will e-race his wheel bolt during the event. I will win. Then everyone will love me because I'm the best, the richest, the most clever and most powerful being on the planet—and I always win!" With his make-believe crowd still cheering him on, he said, "Thank you, thank you. Yes, yes. I know. I truly am better than everyone else!"

That was the plan, and E-racer resented it. He rolled his eyes and said, "It's getting stuffy in here."

CHAPTER FOUR

SWEPT AWAY

Far below at the orchanvilly track, a dizzying twirling session came to an end. Deluxe staggered away as RV let her down. He wobbled a bit, trying to gain his balance. She couldn't help but giggle when she saw him. He actually looked quite funny on his one wheel.

"Whoa," said Deluxe as she reached out to steady him. She gave him a quick kiss on the cheek and said, "RV, you're so cute! You look just like a blue bowling pin!"

It was true. RV looked just like a blue bowling pin that had been hit by a bowling ball and was slowly getting ready to fall down.

Deluxe suddenly remembered that she had to be at class.

"I'm going to be late! I have to go. Thank you, though. This was so much fun," she said. She quickly ran off and shouted, "Bye, RV. Bye!"

RV was stunned. *Did that really just happen?* He reached up and gently touched the spot where she had kissed him on the cheek.

"I think she likes me," he whispered. Thoughts of hope flooded his being. His eyes brightened and his heart raced. "This is good!"

He took off around the orchanvilly field like there was no tomorrow. Every time he thought of her, he was energized all over again. RV considered all that had happened and quieted down. But then he questioned his hasty exuberance. "Wait a minute … a blue bowling pin?"

Perhaps Deluxe still only liked him as a friend. His hopes were down, but at least he was the only one aware of his impulsive enthusiasm. He shrugged it off. He was used to being just friends with Deluxe. So what if he his hopes had risen for a minute?

RV arrived back at the place where Deluxe had left him and saw a coin on the ground. Puzzled, he picked it up to examine it. It was the gold coin he had given her at the café.

Instinctively, he became concerned and gathered his thoughts. Instead of going home, he decided to make sure that Deluxe had made it to her class. He rolled down the pathway towards the beach and saw her orchanvilly lying on the sand. It must have fallen from her hair. Several footprints headed towards the water and ended near the shore.

RV looked out at the aqua blue water and solemnly whispered, "Something's not right."

CHAPTER FIVE

BOMBOOZLED

A periscope from a submersible poked its head out of the water several yards off the shore of Old Castle Island. The periscope turned one way and then the other. It looked quite silly as it twisted. Then the sub emerged from the water and rested at a small island dock. A hatch on top opened. At first, only muffled voices came from the opening. Then a short person with a rather large, red, very round head climbed out of the craft. It was Bombman.

Bombman was the villainous protégé of Major Tomm. He had been given his name for an obvious reason: he had a cherry bomb for a head. (Seriously, his head was really a cherry bomb.) He was fixated on blowing things up and had a secret wish to be a superhero. But there was one problem:

he was not a good guy. In fact, Bombman was a very, very bad guy. Nevertheless, he continued to pretend and wore a superhero outfit with yellow tights and an orange and black cape. He was even able to fly like a superhero, but only for a few minutes at a time.

Unfortunately, Bombman might have been super in many ways, but he was the furthest thing from a hero. He had worked alongside Major Tomm doing many diabolical deeds and was now in the middle of kidnapping Deluxe—just as the Major had instructed him.

Bombman stood on the dock, reached back into the submersible, and pulled out Deluxe. Her hands were tied behind her back and her mouth was covered with a bandana. Two metallic hands from inside the sub pushed her out of the hatch, and she clumsily stepped onto the dock.

The metallic hands belonged to Smokescreen, the subservient associate of Bombman. He was a tall, slender, metallic droid who happened to be very good-natured. One would wonder why Smokescreen had ever become involved with Bombman and Major Tomm. He was not mean or cruel, he did not like hurting others, and he did not care about being important. But Smokescreen was programmed to serve someone, and it had become his duty to serve Bombman.

Smokescreen spoke in a very formal manner and always sounded overly polite. He skittishly attempted to get Bombman's attention.

"Sir, I must insist that you listen to me. I believe we have an intruder."

Smokescreen was convinced that someone or something was out on the water and had followed them to the island. He didn't realize that while his master hardly paid attention to him, Deluxe heard every word. Yet, not even his courteous manner comforted her.

Deluxe was terrified. *Would this intruder be dangerous? How could all of this have happened?* She had been having the time of her life with RV, and now she was kidnapped and stranded on Old Castle Island. No one ever came to Old Castle Island. This had been such a sweet day, and now there was no RV to make her feel safe.

Smokescreen repeated the warning and finally got his master's attention.

"Well, if there is someone following us, he won't be following us for long," said Bombman. He was confident because his intuition rarely failed him. He pulled out a remote control device from his pocket, pressed the red button, and pushed Deluxe forward. "Go on, girlie. Move it," he said.

Suddenly, they heard a loud noise. A bomb had gone off in the water. Deluxe and Smokescreen were taken by surprise, and the polite droid immediately held his nose.

"WHEW! What was that?" asked Smokescreen.

Bombman had a sinister smile on his face. "Hee-hee! I dropped a bomb!"

"Oh! That is disgusting," said Smokescreen. The excessively courteous droid held his hand over Deluxe's nose in order to relieve her of the odious vapors. "Here, young missy. You shouldn't have to breathe that!"

"See that out there?" said Bombman as he proudly pointed to a small atomic cloud over the ocean. "That's my bomb, man! Although I have to admit, it *was* a bit of a stink bomb. Hee-hee-hee!"

Smokescreen waved his other hand in front of his nose as if to get rid of the smell.

"Sir, that's just nasty!"

Bombman was delighted with his smelly bomb. "There's more where that came from."

He stopped laughing and his tone of voice changed as he handed the remote to Smokescreen. Bombman was serious when he gave commands.

"Take this! Here is what I want you to do: get rid of that intruder. Do that whole smokescreen thing you do and cover the entire island. Do you know what I mean?"

"Yes sir," said Smokescreen.

He knew what Bombman meant. Smokescreen liked to think of himself as a master of disguises. Perhaps "master of camouflage" would be a better title. However, the only camouflage that had ever been requested was that of a smokescreen. He could run at a relatively high speed and release smoke at the same time, because he was empowered with a special fuel backpack. Seeing through the smoke was difficult for anyone but him. This gave the droid a great advantage; it allowed him to target intruders and not be seen.

There was only one major disadvantage with this maneuver. It caused Smokescreen's interior gears to fill up with a eulosynthetic gel, a gooey substance that was difficult to remove. The gel would usually take an hour or so to liquefy after a run was completed. It was no wonder that Smokescreen cringed at the thought of what he had been ordered to do.

Bombman continued to give orders. "Create the smokescreen so that the intruder can't see anything. Then bomb him with the remote. If all else fails, use this poison arrow pistol on him."

Smokescreen had just been given his most important assignment. It was up to him to defend the island from the intruder, but he searched for an excuse to get out of it. He hated the side effects of this camouflage.

"Aw, sir! Must I really do the smokescreen?" he asked. "Whenever I release smoke, my cogs and wheels get so clogged up that my nose canal is flooded, and it won't stop running. I always end up covered with ..." He stopped and blushed beet red, embarrassed in front of Deluxe. He paused and then tried to speak again. "Well, what I mean to say is ... I always end up with ... uh ..."

"SPIT IT OUT, MAN!" shouted Bombman. "What are you trying to say? Are you trying to tell me that your nose runs? I already know that. Your nose runs like a waterfall!"

Smokescreen was overwhelmed. "Please sir ... if you don't mind."

Bombman shook his finger at Smokescreen as if he were teaching a lesson.

It is important to note here that whenever Bombman shook his finger and started to correct anyone, he always began by saying, "There's one thing you need to learn." Then without fail, he finished his lesson by singing his advice. Yes, I said *singing*. On top of that, his songs were completely out of tune.

Bombman's guidance sounded like this, "There's one thing you need to learn, Smokescreen." He continued in an unredeemable melody, " HE WHO does his job, KEEPS his job!" (Try singing that last line very loud and out of tune and you'll get the idea.)

Then Bombman whisked Deluxe up in his arms and flew high to the Old Castle atop the island.

Smokescreen began his run. He moved along at a decent pace, and smoke encircled the entire island rather quickly. This was easy since the island was quite small. However, when he returned to the dock, the intruder in the water was moving closer.

Smokescreen's runny nose bothered him as he awkwardly began to gather ammunition. Soon he was covered with gel. His arms became uncoordinated because they were loaded with sticky gear. Holding the remote control bombing device in one hand and the poison arrow pistol in the other, he managed to push a green button on his chest that electronically lowered a pair of binocular scopes to his eyes. Something out on the water appeared to be coming toward him. He focused his scopes to see more clearly, but all he could see was a *blur of blue*.

Yes, oh yes! It was the *blur of blue* that we have so fondly come to know as RV, the Racer Aardvark, speeding toward Old Castle Island. His wheel joints worked like rudders propelling him on top of the water. He was hardly wet at all!

Standing on the shore, Smokescreen realized that he was in a do-or-die situation. He took a deep breath and prepared for a fight. The remote was capable of firing hundreds of bombs, so he decided to drop them all in sequence. This blue invader would certainly be hit, and more than once, at that. The bombs began to drop.

RV continued to gain momentum as he approached the island. The first bomb dropped several yards away from him. The smelly explosion caused the water to ripple from the hit zone. RV reacted to the surprise attack with an accelerated mental response. First, how would he avoid the bombs? Second, what about the unpredictable waves? Third, how was he was going to handle the smell?

He remained focused. He could sense where the bombs would fall based on their timing, their previous locations, and the vibrations prior to each hit. He dodged them all and zigzagged over the water as if he was making his way through a maze.

As for the swells, he took to riding them like a surfer in a competition, railing against the ruptured waters and challenging them with the grace and ability of a true athlete. He barreled through wet tunnels as he did 360-degree glides in the full motion pipes. He knew in the back of his mind that Deluxe was in trouble, and he had to get through this for her sake.

RV blasted out of a curling crest of water and soared. A whirring sound whizzed past him as he caught air. Again, he balanced himself on the water—and something else whizzed past. It was an arrow. He looked up and saw another arrow headed straight at him. Before he had time to think, he caught it. Another bomb went off, and the waves surged in different directions. A second arrow flew toward him, and he caught that, too.

RV knew he could not give up. He dodged the bombs, surfed the raging waters, and caught the arrows until there were no bombs or arrows left.

Finally, he reached the shore. Without wasting a moment, he traveled along the coast, holding at least a dozen arrows in his hand. Before long, he was able to peer through the smoky air well enough to see the silhouette of Smokescreen fumbling with his equipment on the beach.

Smokescreen was a mess. His cogs and wheels were completely clogged, and his nose was running. The more he tried to clean himself up, the worse his condition grew.

RV could not stop himself from laughing quietly. *This guy needs help!* he thought. He tucked all the arrows under his arm and opened the secret compartment in his belly.

All aardvarks on Zein have a secret compartment in their belly similar to the pouches that kangaroos have on Earth. However, an aardvark's belly can hold a great quantity of wonderful things.

RV decided to relieve the poor fellow's drainage problem. He pulled out several tissues, fashioned them into paper airplanes, and aimed.

Smokescreen staggered unsteadily, frustrated that he had not conquered the intruder on behalf of Bombman. Then a tissue flew toward him; it seemed to stop in thin air right beside his face. He grabbed it.

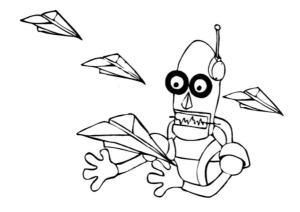

"What's this?" Smokescreen said. He quickly used it to blow his nose and was very relieved.

RV emerged from the edge of the fog and dropped his arrows at the droid's feet. He whipped out tissue after tissue, and his opponent was happy to use them to clean himself.

"You looked like you could use some tissues. Do you need any more?" said RV.

Smokescreen held a tissue close to his nose and said with a tear in his eye, "Sir, you have made it through my smokescreen. You have caught every one of my arrows and dodged all my stink bombs. Sir, you are truly remarkable." He paused and sniffled. "But most extraordinary of all, you have given me—your enemy—something to wipe his boogers with."

"Hey, it's okay," said RV.

Smokescreen was moved deep down to the core of his being. If being programmed to serve someone was his fate, then from this moment forward, he would serve someone new. He would serve this blue aardvark.

"Whatever you ask of me, I will do it for you. From now on, I am Smokescreen, your loyal servant," he said.

This was more than RV wanted or expected, but he smiled and said, "Thank you, Smokescreen. It is very nice to meet you. Maybe you can help me. I need to find my friend, Deluxe. I think she might be in danger."

"Certainly, sir. I know the way," replied Smokescreen. He was happy to take on a cause for his kind new master.

Suddenly, he realized that he didn't even know his new master's name so he asked. "Excuse me sir, your name?"

"RV, the—"

"—Racer Aardvark?" Smokescreen was taken aback.

"That would be me," said RV.

"OH, YES! Oh my! Gollywoggles—yes!" Smokescreen was delighted. He gloated and chattered about RV's reputation. "RV, the Racer Aardvark! Why, they say you are the fastest thing on one wheel. You are the only thing Major Tomm and Bombman talk about."

While Smokescreen basked in the joy of his newly found master, RV was alerted by the mention of Major Tomm.

"Major Tomm? Bombman? Who is Bombman?" he asked.

"Oh dear," was all Smokescreen could say. He grimaced when he thought of the evil plans in store for RV. "Sir, you are truly going to need my help."

CHAPTER SIX

OLD CASTLE ISLAND

Atop the highest mountain on the island stood the Old Castle. It was an ancient structure with large gray stone walls, eerie and intriguing at the same time. It looked like the kind of place you would like to read about in a story, but not one you would want to live in.

Someone, however, was very happy to live there. Bombman looked out the tower window with satisfaction at his newly acquired property.

"At last! My very own city!" he said.

He could see Smokescreen's smoke as it encircled the island, and he got the chills. He could not help but congratulate himself.

"My own city," he shouted again, "over which I have total control!" He threw his fist victoriously into the air. "Yeah, baby! I own a city! I have total control!"

Bombay Island had a nice ring to it. Bombman thought it sounded much better than Old Castle Island. Of course, he would have to change all the signs and such, but it would be worth it. He imagined all the things he could do with his own city. He could build up the tourist industry since the island had an ancient castle. Promoting the island would be like promoting himself. "Bombay" and "Bombman" would become trademarks— yes, even icons. He could think of many ways to use the word "Bomb" to advertise business on the island. He would follow Major Tomm's example and name everything after himself.

While Bombman gazed out and gloated, Deluxe sat nearby, strapped to a chair. She was terrified and found it difficult to think. Trying to calm her nerves, she told herself that perhaps some good would come of this situation. She was comforted by the fact that Bombman had not harmed her physically; however, the fear of what *might* happen continued to creep through her mind. There was also the ghastly smell. What a predicament! Deluxe was trapped with Bombman whose foul odor had a way of lurking in the air wherever he went.

Neither of them knew that several floors beneath them, RV and Smokescreen had crept up the circular stairway to Bombman's chambers. RV looked back at Smokescreen and urged him to be quiet.

"Ssshhh! He's up there. I can hear him," said RV.

He glided to the top of the stairwell and peeked around the corner. Bombman's chamber was furnished with state-of-the-art technological equipment. In fact, it looked very much like a control tower full of machinery and communication devices.

A vu-screen materialized before his eyes. RV had never seen such a large vu-screen. He looked around the room. When he saw Deluxe strapped to a chair, he winced with anger, but he suppressed his emotions in order to figure out a solution. He knew it wouldn't do any good to rush in on Bombman. He decided to lure the villain away from Deluxe in order to take him on. It would be the best way to keep her out of harm's way.

The big screen was so large that it practically filled the room. At first there was only static, but after a few moments, Major Tomm's face became visible.

"Bombman … Come in, Bombman," called the Major.

The cherry-bomb-headed accomplice responded immediately and approached the screen.

"Yes, Major. I am here," Bombman said.

"Do you have her?" asked Major Tomm.

"Yes, of course," said Bombman.

RV learned that not only had Deluxe been kidnapped, but Major Tomm was responsible for the dreadful act. He continued to eavesdrop on their conversation

"Fantastic!" said Major Tomm. "Now I want you to send a ransom note to that Racer Aardvark. Tell him his waitress friend is being held hostage. If he wants her back, he must bring you the First Place Trophy from the Unicycle Division of the Major Races. Got that?"

RV's eyes just about bugged out of his head! This was worse than he ever could have imagined. Now he understood that Major Tomm was the one who had sent all those letters and vu-screen messages to make him enter the Major Races. He guessed that the random newspaper ads and articles he'd found were also part of the Major's coercive tactics. But kidnapping Deluxe just to get him to race? Well, that seemed plain stupid! What sort of greed would motivate someone to kidnap a person? RV pondered all this as he listened to the Major and Bombman converse with one another.

"Yes sir," said Bombman. "I just have one question. You and I both know that you are going to win the race, and that the Racer Aardvark will never see the trophy. What should I do with the girlie here?"

RV realized that the Major had devised a scheme to make him race and lose, but what came next really troubled him.

"Do whatever you like with her," said the Major. "I don't care. Use her for target practice."

Whoa! That did it. This was wicked! The Major and Bombman were laughing. RV looked at Deluxe's face. She was terrified.

He waited and watched until she happened to glance towards him. Immediately, he raised his index finger to his lips and mouthed, "Ssshhh!" Seeing RV, Deluxe felt somewhat relieved.

"Oh, speaking of target practice," said Bombman, proceeding with his report, "someone followed us to the island. Don't worry, though. I had Smokescreen bring out the bombs on him. Hee-hee-hee. Blasted away, baby!"

This was the absolute worst thing that Bombman could have said to Major Tomm. It set him off into hysterics.

"You bungling bubblehead!" shouted the Major. "You'd better not have blasted the aardvark. My whole show will be spoiled if I don't get to race against him."

RV shook his head. So that was it. It was all about the show. What about Deluxe? Didn't her life mean more than a show? Major Tomm was a raving lunatic. His deranged mind had determined that RV would race and lose to make the Major Races a good show—no matter what the cost. The Major was bonkers—completely whacko!

RV wheeled back down the stairwell and found Smokescreen waiting for him faithfully. He knew Smokescreen was well acquainted with Bombman since he had been his slave for many years.

RV said, "Is there anything you can tell me about this Bombman that might help me? You know, like … what are his weaknesses?"

Smokescreen struggled to come up with an answer. Unsure of himself, his reply sounded more like a question.

"He has a short fuse?"

RV was quiet.

The polite droid gave it more thought. Then he said excitedly, "He's mean! He's wicked and he's very, very evil."

"He's evil, huh?" RV was as calm as a doctor giving a

remedy for the common cold. "Well, then he'll fall into his own trap."

Smokescreen was perplexed by this remark.

RV confidently reassured him, repeating, "He'll fall into his own trap."

"Sir, how do you know that?" Smokescreen asked.

He thought RV had some kind of secret knowledge that made him confident of Bombman's fate. This was not the case at all. RV simply had a keen grasp of the natural laws of Zein.

"Listen, Smokescreen," RV explained, "anyone who devises evil plans for others will eventually fall into some kind of trap of his own making."

Smokescreen quietly listened and learned while RV geared up for yet another challenge.

In a playfully sarcastic tone, RV said, "Let's just see if I can speed up that process for old Bombman! Find a place to hide, Smokescreen, and wait for me."

"Yes sir. Whatever you say," said the metallic droid. He turned and looked around for a way to disguise himself.

RV climbed the stairs towards Bombman's control chambers. After a few steps, he glanced back at his new friend.

"Hey, Smokescreen," he said in a loud whisper. "How's your runny nose?"

Smokescreen sniffed twice, felt his nose, and reported back.

"Doing okay."

"Good," said RV, and he continued up the stairs.

Smokescreen was awestruck. His new master showed concern for him even while trying to free Deluxe. RV had made such a profound impression on him that it was as if he was becoming a new person.

RV sneaked through the door and stood just inside the control chambers. Then things happened fast. He decided to startle Bombman by showing up unexpectedly. He wanted his opponent to chase him, so he challenged the smelly fellow by whistling through his flute nose, as if to say, *Catch me if you can.*

"Hey, you're that Racer Aardvark!" shouted the cherry-bomb-headed scoundrel.

Seeing RV come out of nowhere, Bombman was definitely taken aback. He felt like a fool, and he didn't like feeling like a fool. His instant remedy for the situation was to try to capture the aardvark, and he immediately jumped in pursuit. He had taken the bait—the chase was on!

RV whizzed down the stairwell and passed Smokescreen, who had disguised himself as an armored statue. Bombman pushed a button on his remote control to engage the electric doors. The *blur of blue* was in full force, speeding down several flights of stairs. Just as the heavy doors came crashing down to trap him, he rolled under them.

Bombman ran back to the control chambers and turned on the big vu-screen to monitor RV's location in the castle. He pushed the button on the remote again to shut the entry gate and trap the Racer Aardvark inside, but it was too late. RV was already outside the castle, whizzing down the road.

Bombman flipped out! He slithered his fingers together in a wicked, spider-like fashion and vowed his personal retaliation.

"I'll get him! I'll get him!" Bombman shouted, jumping up and down. "There's one thing that aardvark needs to learn." (Oh, no! Here comes the out-of-tune singing.) "HE WHO … controls the city … hee-hee … KNOWS WHERE all the secret weapons are!"

This was Bombman's way of yelling CHARGE! He lost his temper and chased RV without any thought or plan. He had no idea what he would do when he caught up with him.

The fog from Smokescreen's run around the island had evaporated, and the air was crisp and clear again. The familiar *blur of blue* zoomed along, with Bombman not far behind him. RV slowed down to let his rival think he was gaining ground, and Bombman edged closer. But the racer aardvark just poked fun at him, whistling through his flute nose, and then took off like a bolt of lightning.

Bombman was mad! He was not going to let that aardvark get away with making a fool of him. After all, this was Bombay Island now! This was *his* island, and he knew where all the bombs and booby traps were hidden. He pointed his finger into the air as if he was about to make another one of his legendary out-of-tune declarations.

There was no declaration, though. Bombman had a clever new idea instead. The aardvark would eventually try to get back to Deluxe in the castle. Why should Bombman chase him when he could set traps and wait for him? He stopped in front of the rock wall of a mountainside, dug a pit, and covered the pit with a net. To camouflage the trap, he switched on his portable vu-screen and made it display a road winding into the distance—but it was only an onscreen image that concealed the net, the pit, and the rocky wall.

RV flew past Bombman and disappeared into the vu-screen.

Bombman scratched his head and wondered, "How did he do that?"

He tried to run into the vu-screen the way RV did, but he merely punched through the screen and smacked into the rocky mountain wall—only to land in the pit! He was so angry that his little red head glowed and smoked!

RV stood across the way smiling. He had used his own vu-screen to play a hologram image of himself racing into Bombman's winding road. He let the hologram image race back and forth as Bombman dug himself out of the pit. Then RV flute-nose whistled and took off.

"*GGRRRRR!* That's it!" Bombman brushed himself off, climbed out, and said, "I've had it! I don't care about any … *ggrrrrr!* … Major Races. It's time to bring out the bombs!" He completely lost his temper and decided to step up his retaliation tactics.

"There's one thing that aardvark needs to learn," he said. (Oh no, here we go again with the out of tune singing.) "HE WHO … owns the bombs … GETS TO … USE the bombs!"

Bombman found another hiding place where RV would likely pass, and he waited for him. When the *blur of blue* sped passed him, he threw cherry bombs in every direction. The bombs exploded and left so many large holes that Bombman was trapped—surrounded by holes! If he took a step in any direction, he might easily fall into one of them

RV rolled in as closely as possible. "Had enough?" he asked. Then he whistled and took off again.

But Bombman had *not* had enough, and he was getting sick of hearing that aardvark's whistle! He was intoxicated with rage, and his only thought was to find and destroy the aardvark. He knew better and more ingenious traps. If he combined some of them with more precise bombing strategies, he would be good to go. He would certainly be able to destroy that pesky aardvark once and for all.

Bombman was out in full force now. He painted a section of road with special mega-cohesive glue and pushed out a guided missile on a rolling cart. The cart was heavy, and moving it took the wind out of him. He leaned back for a moment. *Whoosh!* He had accidentally leaned against one of the levers and turned on the missile. What a surprise! The jet-firing rockets almost hit him in the behind! To make matters worse, the missile broke out of its carrier cart, and he had to chase it.

Despite the mishap, Bombman was able to get the missile on course using his remote control. The jet-firing projectile gained momentum as it traveled up a winding mountain road, and soon it was on the heels of the *blur of blue.* Bombman flew and caught up with his elusive opponent. RV looked straight at him and gave him a wink and, of course, a whistle.

"Aha!" exclaimed Bombman when he heard the insulting whistle. "This time he thinks he's getting away, but just wait!"

There was a large sign on the road with a big red arrow that pointed to the right. RV took the detour. But the guided missile didn't follow him—it went in the opposite direction. There was a hidden cave at the end of the road, and RV disappeared into it. RV, the Racer Aardvark, had finally fallen into Bombman's trap. Bombman climbed to a high rock where he had hidden a stash of zapignite explosives. He lit a bundle of zapignite, threw it into the cave, and sat back on a rock to wait, smiling. But … there was no explosion.

Bombman peered into the cave, wondering why nothing had happened. *Oh, no! Now what?* he thought. A loud, angry growl came from inside. Bombman continued to stare into the cave out of curiosity.

Suddenly, a giant hand reached out and snatched him by the head. It was a Cartesian grizmot—a combination of bear and droid (in earthling terminology), and much larger than the other creatures on Zein. This particular grizmot was very angry as he came out of his cave. He grabbed Bombman by the head the way a player would grab a basketball, dribbled him several times, and threw him for a long shot. As Bombman hurled through the air, he did six somersaults.

RV was standing on a rock high above the cave. He held out an anderlies net to catch him, and Bombman swooped down into it—but he broke right through it and landed feet first in the glue that he had painted on the road. He struggled to break away, but he could not budge. He was inescapably stuck in the glue.

Well, it didn't end there. The guided missile, which had been perfectly timed, was headed directly toward Bombman. It flew over his head and lit the fuse on his cherry bomb head. Stuck in the glue and trying to get free while the short fuse burned, he was in a serious dilemma. He was literally a live bomb!

RV whistled again as if to say, *Do you still want to catch me?*

Even though Bombman was helpless, he continued to try to intimidate RV, shouting absurdly, "Get off of my property! This is my city. I have total control. I am the boss of everything!"

"Okay, boss," said RV with a smirk. He shook his finger and mimicked Bombman's infamous, out-of-tune pronouncement. "You know, Bombman, there's one thing you needed to learn. HE WHO controls his temper has more power than HE WHO controls a city."

Bombman's fuse burned shorter and shorter until finally—he exploded! Cherry bomb head and all! With a very loud *KABOOM!*

CHAPTER SEVEN

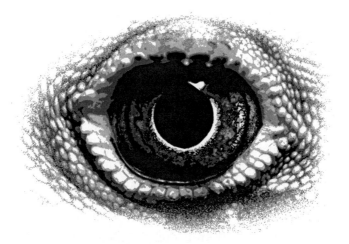

CREATURES
OF THE UNDER

RV hurried back to the castle, whizzed up the stairwell, and found Smokescreen still disguised as an armored statue. Accustomed to taking orders, his new friend had done nothing since he received the last one. He might have waited for RV in that stairwell forever if he hadn't been ordered to move.

RV grabbed him and said, "Let's go!"

They entered Bombman's chambers. RV loosened the bandana from Deluxe's mouth and untied her from the chair. She looked frightened.

"Deluxe, you are free now. Are you all right?" RV asked, gently patting her head.

"Yes, thank you," she said. "Did you hear Major Tomm talking to Bombman on the big screen? I didn't think I would live through this."

She noticed Smokescreen and her heart started to race.

RV said, "Don't worry. This is Smokescreen. He's with us now. He helped me rescue you."

Smokescreen walked over to Deluxe and saw how concerned she was. Her pretty little face was tense with anxiety. His heart melted; he was ashamed to have been part of Bombman's evil scheme. He wanted to put her mind at rest, but he knew that she had no reason to trust him.

Deluxe stood up and took Smokescreen's hand. She was not angry with him. In fact, she treated him much more kindly than he deserved. He understood why RV would risk his life for her.

Smokescreen said, "I am so sorry, young missy. I knew Bombman was evil, but I was his slave. I would have done my best to protect you."

Smokescreen's allegiance was sealed from this point on, and he vowed to protect his two new friends.

RV finally said, "It looks like Major Tomm will do the unthinkable to get me to race against him in the Major Races." His next statement really shocked them. "So I will save him the trouble."

"What?" said Deluxe and Smokescreen simultaneously.

RV explained. "Look, I don't care about those races." He glanced at Deluxe. "But I do care about you. So I'll give him what he wants. I'll race against him. That way, he'll have no reason to come after you. Come on, let's go."

RV's decision surprised Smokescreen, but he was confident that RV knew what he was doing. He relaxed a bit. Then he noticed some food on Bombman's desk.

"Hmm … snacks," said Smokescreen as he packed several goodies into his backpack. "I might need these."

When he turned around, he realized that RV and Deluxe had left without him, and he set off to look for them.

Smokescreen caught up with the others at the submersible dock. The dock and the sub were wrecked. The whole place had been blown up in the bomb fest between Smokescreen and RV.

"Are there any other vehicles on the island to carry us to the mainland?" asked RV.

The subservient droid looked around and saw an old weatherworn shed several yards away.

"Sir, there is the bubble," he said.

RV had no idea what he was talking about. "The bubble? What's the bubble?"

"This way sir," said Smokescreen as he led them to the old shed.

They pulled back two large decrepit doors and saw a globe-shaped vehicle made of a shatterproof transparent material.

"This is the bubble," explained Smokescreen. "It was used to transport goods many years ago from the island to the mainland. Sir, it travels on a monorail system under the ground and the sea. It's not really meant for people, and it hasn't been used in over a century. I suppose we could try it and see what happens. We could probably use it to get to the mainland, but it would only take us to the Braggadocio Hole."

"Interesting," said RV as he looked inside to check things out.

Smokescreen said, "The monorail might have been damaged during the bombing."

RV shook his head. "No, those were surface bombs. The monorail is too far below the surface for those bombs to have affected it."

Once he ascertained that the equipment was not defective and the level of azidien was adequate for them to breathe, he decided to try it and jumped in.

Deluxe and Smokescreen lowered themselves into the bubble and sat beside him. RV fired up the equipment. It shook several times, before it rapidly headed downward, falling faster and faster as it gained momentum. A few seconds later, the vehicle pushed forward with a jerk and bolted through an underground cave. Finally, it shot out into the Under.

The Under is what many on Zein had come to refer to as the world beneath the sea. According to legend, unknown beings dwelled in the Under. They had vacated their cities, but after the passage of centuries, the homes and buildings were still intact.

The journey from Old Castle Island to the mainland was not long, and traveling in the Under turned out to be an exceptional adventure. The bubble moved smoothly and speedily through the waters, and the light rays of the three suns' illumined the surroundings for all to see. They passed exquisite creatures and plants as they traveled! The vehicle took several unexpected fun turns; it was like an underwater roller coaster ride.

When Deluxe looked back at the island, her mouth dropped in awe. "Look at that! It's a dinosadroid!" she said.

RV and Smokescreen were utterly astonished. What they all thought was Old Castle Island was really the back of a gigantic underwater dinosadroid! .

A dinosadroid was very similar to a dinosaur on Earth; however, the creatures on Zein were hydraulic droids. This one was extraordinary. It had huge reptilian legs and a long spiny tail. Its large head rested on the ocean floor, and the hump of its back made up Old Castle Island. There were other smaller islands nearby that were also dinosadroids.

Smokescreen eased some of the tension, saying, "Not to worry, young missy. These are petrified dinosadroids. They turned into rock centuries ago."

Just as he finished speaking, the bubble jerked. It had hit the head of another underwater dinosadroid.

"I thought this would take us to the Braggadocio Hole," said RV.

"Sir, it is supposed to, but it appears that we are stuck," said Smokescreen.

Suddenly, Deluxe screamed at the top of her lungs. She had seen the head of yet another dinosadroid through the window. They had run into dinosadroids that were neck to neck, and next to her window, a gigantic eye opened wide!

She panicked and could not move. With one more jerk, the bubble was thrust into the open mouth of one of the great beasts.

Deluxe grabbed RV. "Weren't these creatures supposed to be petrified?" she said.

As it turned out, the dinosadroids *were* petrified. Designers had found a way to use their large backs for island mass and their hydraulic capabilities for lifting purposes. Dinosadroids had air holes very much like whales have on Earth. In fact, the petrified dinosadroid had been engineered to load or "swallow" the bubble. This was part of the transport system that delivered goods from the island to the surface of the mainland. The creature swallowed the vehicle and spewed it out of its ancient air hole, which, as it turned out, was the famous geyser known as the Braggadocio Hole.

Many tourists were visiting the Braggadocio Hole that particular day. When a giant bubble shot out of it, they were awestruck. Everyone had thought of the faithful geyser as a family attraction; no one ever suspected that it was actually the air hole of a giant petrified underground dinosadroid.

The bubble landed a short distance away from the geyser, and all the tourists, tour guides, and park security guards rushed to see what happened. The top opened and RV, Smokescreen, and Deluxe popped their heads out. Several people recognized RV, and there was a huge commotion. Tourists vu-screened the phenomenon. It was quite an event. After all, this kind of thing did not happen every day, even on Zein.

The trio were glad they had landed near the Braggadocio Hole because everyone there was so helpful. Several bystanders were excited when they found out that RV was going to race in the Major Races.

The park guide allowed them to spend the night there, providing a much needed rest after their great adventure. He fed them dinner and cooked them breakfast in the morning. He also told them how to get to the Major's business building.

"Take the main road by the coast, travel north, and then just follow the signs. The road will take you right to Major Tomm," said the park guide.

Deluxe and RV felt quite refreshed. Smokescreen managed all right too, but he never seemed to get enough to eat. It was a good thing that his backpack was full of snacks.

And so they started walking—except for RV, of course. He rolled.

CHAPTER EIGHT

THE GNARLY FOREST

Smokescreen munched loudly on his snacks, and the noise slightly annoyed Deluxe.

"Would you like some, young missy?" Smokescreen asked.

She shook her head. "No thanks."

They came to a fork in the road and saw two signs. One sign said "Major City" and the other said "Gnarly Forest." The way to go seemed obvious. However, their interest was peaked when they got close to the forest. Dark clouds rolled in, and the trees looked ominous and foreboding. They had huge trunks and twisted, intertwined branches that formed a net-like canopy. From time to time, winderts flew through the trees. The forest had an eerie magnetism.

RV, Deluxe, and Smokescreen were enchanted by the Gnarly Forest's irresistible lure. They stood frozen in their tracks, staring. The trees looked peculiar, as if they were breathing, and a large one near them slowly opened its eyes. Several other trees opened their eyes, too, and moved their twisted branches like arms. When the large tree opened its mouth wide, it let out a blood-curdling laugh, and hundreds of winged creatures flew out and up into the sky.

"WHOA! Déjà vu!" said Smokescreen. "I feel like I've been here before."

The Gnarly Forest was chilling, creepy, and dangerous. Smokescreen thought he was reliving a past experience. Had his imagination overtaken him? Wait a minute! What was that? A windert flew right past his nose. They heard another loud screech and looked up to see one of the old trees staring angrily at them. Several giant ratchulas scurried away as an overgrown spyderoid peaked out from behind one of the trees.

RV took the lead and comforted them. "Well, we definitely don't want to go through the Gnarly Forest," he said.

The others were relieved that they were going to keep their distance from the cursed woodland.

RV continued. "I think Major Tomm lives in Major City. Yes, that makes sense. I say, let's go to Major City."

Deluxe agreed and clung to his arm. Smokescreen tried to hide the fact that he really was afraid and said, "That sounds like an excellent plan, sir."

They heard another loud, eerie screech. Smokescreen forgot his illusions of ever having been there and scrambled to the front of the group to get away from the forest as quickly as possible.

CHAPTER NINE

MEET THE MAJOR

The Major Income business building was a luxurious skyscraper in the central district of Major City. In the penthouse office, Major Tomm was upset because the big screen communicator was showing nothing but static.

"Bombman!" said the Major. "Can you hear me? Come in, Bombman. Come in!"

He looked at E-racer angrily and picked him up by the neck.

"E-racer! Did you do something? Did you accidentally e-race Bombman? You're always accidentally e-racing things. If I find out …"

His secretary interrupted him on the intercom. "Major Tomm, there is an RV, the Racer Aardvark, here to see you."

The Major dropped E-racer on the floor like a hot potato. "What?" Major Tomm asked. "What did you say?"

"Sir, I said, there is an RV, the Racer Aardvark here to see you."

The Major was shocked. He had been so obsessed with wicked schemes to get the aardvark to race at the Major Races that he could hardly believe RV was at his door.

"Tell him to wait right there," Major Tomm said. "I'll send E-racer down to meet him."

"Yes sir," the secretary replied.

Major Tomm turned to E-racer, baffled. "I don't know how this happened, and at this point, I don't really care. I just want that aardvark to race against me in the Major Races. Go downstairs and bring him up."

"Y-y-yes, Major," said E-racer. He hopped into the elevator and pushed the button to the lobby. As the doors closed behind him, he heard Major Tomm yell, "Make sure you tell him how wonderful I am!"

E-racer fretfully tried to figure out what good things he could say about Major Tomm. Finally he wrote on his notepad, "We're friends." Then he thought about it for a minute.

"N-n-no," he said and quickly crossed it off.

He could not think of anything good to say. The more he thought about it, the more he realized that he was never able to please the Major, no matter how hard he tried. He scratched his head with this revelation, and the elevator doors opened.

RV and the rest of the group waited in the lobby. It had taken them an entire day to get there because they had traveled by foot. Even though Smokescreen's snacks had filled their tummies, they were exhausted from the journey. But they were all anxious to see the Major.

"Let's do this," said RV.

E-racer nervously looked at them and said, "Y-y-yes. C-c-come in, come in."

The pen flew out of his hand and fell to the ground. Deluxe picked up the pen and handed it to him.

"Here you go. You dropped this," she said.

E-racer stopped in his tracks. Someone had actually done something nice for him. He looked smitten and sheepishly smiled at Deluxe.

"Y-y-you're n-n-nice," he said.

RV's heart was very protective when it came to Deluxe. He was a bit jealous and did not appreciate E-racer talking to her that way.

"Hey, guy! We're here to see the Major," he said as he gently pulled Deluxe away.

The elevator doors closed, and E-racer pushed the button for the top floor.

"Oh, y-y-yes," he said. "I-I-I'll tell you all about th-th-the Major … all about the Major."

E-racer tried to give a good report, but instead, he spilled out stories about his employer's peculiar behavior, and how he always looked down on him. The little green apprentice also revealed that he thought his boss was going insane.

Major Tomm was standing just outside the elevator when the doors opened, and he heard what E-racer was saying. Extremely displeased, he picked the apprentice up by the back of the neck and dangled him at his side.

The Major cleared his throat and said, "Yes, yes, I think that will be quite enough. I'll handle it from here." He put on an air of phony friendliness. "Welcome! Welcome! RV, the Racer Aardvark, and friends. Welcome to Major Income!"

He tossed E-racer aside and said, "It's wonderful to have you here. Come along and follow me. I'll give you a tour of the place."

RV suspected that the Major was about to spend a lot of time talking about himself.

"I don't mean to be rude," he said, "but we're here because I want to enter the races."

Major Tomm's face lit up with a strange combination of greed and delight.

"That's just marvelous! Come into my office. I'll get the forms for you," he said.

He went to his big desk and handed RV the entry forms. In a deceitful and cunning tone he continued. "Don't be concerned about the disclosure on the bottom of the form. It's just a formality."

RV looked closely at the document and read aloud, "This agreement shall be binding: Failure to perform shall result in *something unpleasant for you* that will benefit Major Tomm."

"You won't regret entering the Major Races," said the Major with such childlike enthusiasm that it was hard to believe he was so devious. "The Unicycle Race is definitely going to be the most spectacular event of the year. They're calling it the Unies. It's brand new, you know."

Smokescreen was still getting used to the idea that he was no longer a servant. His newfound freedom made him curious about the world around him, and he had a lot to learn.

He noticed a sign above large double doors that read, Proton Showroom.

"Oh, my! What is this?" he said in his typical polite manner.

Major Tomm smiled so enthusiastically that he forgot RV was signing the entry forms. "Well, now! Let me show you what's behind those doors," he said.

He slid open the doors to reveal a large parlor. An elaborate zyno player stood in front of a giant painting of Proton, hanging on the wall. (A zyno player is something like a grand piano.) The room was filled with Proton collectibles such as posters, wheels, decks, banners, and photographs.

Proton was a legendary champion on Zein. Everyone in the room knew of the Proton enigma. He was a skeletal creature, but brilliant in appearance. Partly droid, with wings made of laser light pinions that glowed in the dark, he lived in the heart of the Gnarly Forest and was famous for the sport known as "skate."

(Believe it or not, *skate* on Zein is almost identical to the earthly sport called skateboarding. To this day, many sources claim that skateboards were originally made in an "alien workshop.")

Perhaps that was where the interplanetary transfer of the concept of skateboarding occurred. This has never been proven, but along with the theory of time travel, it could explain the existence of skateboarding on the two planets, thousands of light years apart. Of course, when Zeinian skaters catch air, it means something quite different than it does on Earth.)

As a youngster, RV was inspired when he saw Proton's exceptional ability on wheels. The wheels were similar to the one his father had made for him. RV's constant imitation of the famous athlete contributed to his advancement in wheel skills far beyond what anyone ever expected.

Now here he was in a room with a crazy guy who shared the same appreciation for Proton. It quickly became obvious that Major Tomm's feelings had gone beyond admiration; he was obsessed with the athlete.

In an almost dreamy voice, the Major said, "This is my Proton Showroom. I have more collectibles than anyone on the planet."

In the center of the room, a skate wheel was displayed under a lighted glass dome like a sculpture or expensive jewelry exhibit. Major Tomm looked at the sparkling wheel and said, "This is my latest addition."

He took the wheel from under the glass and began to dance while singing homage to Proton. He held the wheel as if he was in love with it. The Major jumped on top of the zyno player, rolled the wheel up one arm, and rotated it down the other. He tossed it into the air and bounced it off his back.

"This is Proton's newest wheel," said Major Tomm, holding it next to his cheek. "He just finished designing it. It's not even on the market yet. In fact, he left early this morning to meet with his manufacturers on the other side of the planet, but still found time to personally give this one to me!"

RV interrupted. "This is all very interesting, but I came to enter the races. I've completed the entry forms, and now we have to leave."

Deluxe nodded her head in agreement.

Major Tomm was distracted by the interruption. He would have preferred to continue boasting about the wheel. Instead, he said, "Oh, yes. You will need to use the practice area to get prepared for the races tomorrow." He looked around as if he were thinking to himself. "I'll tell you what … I'll show you where it is and give you the rest of the tour on the way. It's no fun having guests if you don't get to show off your stuff!"

CHAPTER TEN

ODDITY-BOTS

"This way!" Major Tomm said lyrically as he led his guests toward the elevator.

He looked odd prancing down the hallway and boasting of his future projects. The area was filled with schematics displayed on the walls and three-dimensional renderings of various products, buildings, and inventions. He pointed at a thin, flat apparatus with a shiny surface, leaning against the wall.

"See that there?" he said. "That's an ASP."

He ran towards it and lifted it up so his guests would have a better view. Colorful graphics decorated one side and an image of a serpentoid appeared on the other.

"This is an all season plank," said the Major proudly. "I just invented this, and it should be ready for the Major Races next year."

Of course, Major Tomm had never invented a thing, but he loved to take all the credit.

The ASP was a new kind of sports equipment. Beside it was a large display with drawings and measurements. The Major strutted toward the plans and gladly explained them to his audience.

"You see, there are two panels—one holds liquid droxiden and the other holds a special azidienated fuel." He pointed to an image of a rider in mid-air and said, "The rider starts down a hill, and the motion causes the fuel to activate, which freezes the liquid in the bottom panel. Wallah! This causes fusion between the plank and the terrain, and it simulates nuclear qualities like those of a sled on frozen droxiden. One can ride the plank on different types of terrain in all kinds of weather. This can be a year-round sport. We can build our own indoor-outdoor parks and make lots of money. It will be a wonderful addition to the Major Races next year."

It was a good idea, but RV, Deluxe, and Smokescreen felt sorry for the poor fellow who had invented the thing and who was being ripped off.

The doors opened and they stepped into the elevator. The tour was certainly entertaining, but Major Tomm was so peculiar. He seemed more like a cartoon character than a real person. Even though he treated his guests like royalty, they all knew his true evil intentions.

The elevator descended several levels and opened to a floor that housed hundreds of droids. They were all shaped like large silver and white eggs with thick robotic arms. Every one of them had a number on its back. They had no legs; instead, they glided along on small rollers. The trio felt as if they were walking through a warehouse full of busy, people-sized, mechanical eggs.

"Take a look," said Major Tomm as they strolled through the factory area.

"Odd-it-y bod-it-y! Odd-it-y bod-it-y," the workers chanted.

"These are oddity-bots," said the Major, "They're worker droids and they can be found in every department of Major Income. These particular oddity-bots are building the famous Cookinaide. You know, the kitchen that does everything. It cooks, washes dishes, sets the table, and it even cleans up the dining area."

The Cookinaide factory was indeed a perfectly clean, work-friendly scene with carefully spaced workplaces and bare, colorless walls. It looked like a sanitized surgical unit in a hospital.

The silver and white workers hummed in a unified chant as they welded gears, fastened bolts, and tested equipment parts. The finished product was a fully equipped kitchen that was able to do every chore automatically.

The aroma of freshly baked food filled the air. In another section of the factory, several oddity-bots were testing the cooking capabilities of a new Cookinaide. Smokescreen could not help but follow the marvelous scent of warm baked goods. He pushed through the swinging doors into a large room.

"Oh my!" he exclaimed.

RV and Deluxe followed him, stunned. An enormous sunken mixing bowl was situated in the middle of the room. What was so unexpected was that two oddity-bots, numbered "Four-Two" and "Six-Five," were inside the bowl and they appeared to be wrestling in the batter. These oddity-bots had replaced their rollers with a huge motorized mixing paddle. They looked like giant mud-wrestling cake mixers. Batter flew in all directions from their spinning paddles until the oddity-bots released their hold on each other. Then the whole process started over again.

All Deluxe could say was, "What in the world … ?"

Several other oddity-bots surrounded the mixing bowl and threw vroot at the wrestlers, which would hit them every so often. Vroot on Zein was similar to fruit and vegetables on Earth. Anything edible that grew in the ground was vroot.

"Can I try that?" said Smokescreen.

He grabbed a handful and flung it at one of the wrestlers. *Smack!* It hit a wrestler right in the head.

"This is fun!" he said. "Sir, you should try this."

RV and Deluxe joined in and threw vroot into the giant mixing bowl.

"You're right!" said RV. "This is really funny."

He reached down and loaded up his arms. Then he sped around the perimeter of the bowl, whipped out vroot, and hit the wrestlers in the process. *Whap, whap, whap!* The vroot flew out of his hands. "Hey guys!" he said. "Check this out." *Whap! Whap! Whap!*

"Did I give you permission to do that?" said the Major in a very intimidating voice.

Everyone froze except RV, who flung his last piece at one of the oddity-bot wrestlers.

"Too late!" he called as it flew through the air.

Major Tomm turned to E-racer and commanded, "Intercept that piece of vroot!"

E-racer pointed his powerful index finger and shot at the flying food. He missed it and hit poor Four-Two instead, who instantly dissolved into crystalline specs and disappeared.

"Did you see that?" Deluxe said to RV. They did not realize that this was exactly what they had seen at the orchanvilly field.

The Major picked E-racer up by the neck, held him in the air, and shook him back and forth. "You're always accidentally e-racing things! These oddity-bots were practicing a new product performance for the Major Races tomorrow, and you've just e-raced one of my most important players!"

He threw E-racer into the giant mixing bowl, and he was covered up to his ears in batter. The rest of the group suddenly felt extremely uncomfortable. They had never seen this side of the Major.

RV said, "I'm sure you'll figure something out."

Major Tomm was completely disgusted. He looked at RV with a half-crazed look in his eyes and began to lecture him.

"You! Apparently, YOU have never been to the Major Races!"

RV shook his head. "No, I can't say that I have."

The Major was insulted. His guests had never been to the Major Races and, therefore, were clueless of all he had produced for this spectacular event.

"This is the Pieod Event (pronounced *pie-odd*)," the Major said in a hostile tone. "It is one of the most famous sideshows at the Major Races. Oddity-bots mix the fillings for the delicious pieod desserts in a wrestling match. Guests throw the vroot (or whatever filling has been mixed) at the oddity-bots—just as you have so freely done here. Afterwards, the pieod desserts are sold all over the park. The only place you can get pieod is at the Major Races. There are small pieod, large pieod, pieod made with all kinds of fillings, and the ever famous vroot-filled frozen ice pieod." The Major's mood had changed, and he became very antisocial. "Get away. Get away from me," he said to his guests.

"Th-th-those are m-m-my favorite," said a small voice behind them.

It was E-racer, cleaning off vroot batter.

"What?" griped Major Tomm.

"I-i-ice pieod! Those are my favorite! I-I-I love ice pieod!" said E-racer.

"Ah, yes. That is true! You really do like ice pieod, don't you?"

Major Tomm laughed. Apparently, E-racer's enthusiasm for ice pieod instantly cheered him up.

"You were really glad when I invented those! They are good, aren't they? Seven-Six!" he shouted. "Bring everyone an ice pieod." The Major was happy again.

Oddity-bot Seven-Six went to another section of the factory to get the treats for Major Tomm and his guests.

Ice pieod sounded good, but Smokescreen still wondered where the warm baked goods were and followed Seven-Six in the hope of finding them. He finally discovered the Cookinaide testing area where several oddity-bots put pastries on conveyor belts, which were headed for the packaging area.

Oddity-bot Eight-Six was there and made various strange noises. He seemed alarmed at Smokescreen's presence at first, but then he held out a tray for him.

"You want pieod?" asked the worker-droid.

Smokescreen thought this oddity-bot was very kind to offer him a treat, and he was delighted.

"Why, yes!" he said. "I most certainly do want pieod. Would you mind putting a few of those into my snack pack?"

Major Tomm led the tour back to the elevator. RV noticed that Smokescreen was missing, and he rolled his way back to look for him.

"Smokescreen! What are you doing?" he said when he finally found him. "Come on, let's go!"

The oddity-bot put the last pieod into the backpack.

"Yes, RV … sir! I'm coming," said Smokescreen, and he ran to catch up with the group. Then he quickly looked back and said, "Thank you … uh … Mr. Odd!"

They entered the elevator again and went down to the basement. The doors opened and Major Tomm said, "This is my fuelsolage garage."

The walls were completely covered with posters of the upcoming unicycle race. It looked like a shrine to the Major's obsessive presumption of future glory.

"This is my latest invention: the Uni-Racer 5000," he boasted as he pointed to a technically advanced one-wheeled vehicle in the center of the room.

"Very nice," said Smokescreen.

They gazed at a magnificent machine. It looked like a combination of a rocket and a race car with one central wheel.

"The Uni-Racer 5000 has a duo-core fuel capacity," said the Major. "If one tank of fuel capsules runs dry, another one is readily available. I love this machine! In fact, I intend to make this vehicle famous by winning the Unicycle Division of the Major Races this year. That means beating you, RV."

"Bring it on!" said RV.

This bold answer unnerved Major Tomm. However, he was sidetracked again by Smokescreen, who was looking at the bins with fuel capsules in them.

"What is this?" asked the ever-fascinated droid.

The Major was still troubled by RV's confidence, but he was always happy to answer any questions that allowed him to talk about himself.

"I'm glad you asked, my inquisitive guest," he said as he walked to a large bin marked *E-racer Gel Capsules*. "This bin holds the fuel that gives E-racer the power to point his index finger at anything and cause it to disintegrate."

He laughed heartily and wanted to show off, so he ordered E-racer to e-race something. He had completely forgotten about the incident with the wrestling oddity-bots upstairs and said, "Go ahead, e-race something."

E-racer was nervous, but at the same time he enjoyed displaying his skills. It made him feel important. At times like this, it almost seemed that the Major was pleased with him. Needless to say, this rarely happened.

Major Tomm took a gear and laid it on an empty section of the floor.

"Go ahead. Shoot it."

E-racer pointed his powerful finger and shot at the gear. It crystallized and then disintegrated.

Major Tomm clapped loudly. "Very good!" he said.

"Th-th-thank you. Th-th-thank you, Major," said his willing apprentice, accepting the applause.

E-racer's congratulatory experience was short-lived because the Major proceeded to correct him.

"You still need to practice. You need a lot of practice. In fact, you should spend the whole afternoon practicing."

Deluxe and RV had seen the gear disappear. They looked at each other, realizing that this was what they had seen in the orchanvilly field. RV didn't like the idea of being disintegrated. He was willing to risk racing against the Major, but he really wanted to keep Deluxe away from harm. He pondered, trying to figure out what to do.

Deluxe, however, was not afraid. She really enjoyed the tour. She liked the Cookinaide and the oddity-bots. She would have liked to watch the pieods while they were being baked, and she certainly thought the ice pieod was tasty. Even the Uni-Racer 5000 was an interesting and beautiful vehicle. She wondered if they would get to ride in it. As she looked at it from every angle, she noticed a small sign on the ground.

"What's this?" she asked. "Did you know that this sign fell off?"

Disgruntled, Major Tomm grabbed the sign from Deluxe. He stuck it on another large bin, covering up the word *Trash*. The new sign read, *Uni-Racer Fuel Capsules*. The Major calmed himself.

"This bin holds the fuel capsules for the Uni-Racer 5000," He said. He fumbled, trying to get the new sign to stick. "I need to get this bin repainted."

"Oh, I see," said Deluxe.

The fuelsolage garage door suddenly opened to the outside world.

"Well, that's the tour!" said Major Tomm. He pointed to the racetrack in the distance. "You can practice on that track over there. I will see you tomorrow at the races. Good luck."

That was it. The Major was done with them—just like that! RV, Deluxe, and Smokescreen went outside, and the fuelsolage garage door slammed shut behind them. It closed so hard that the sign on the uni-racer fuel bin fell off. Once again, the bin said, *Trash*.

CHAPTER ELEVEN

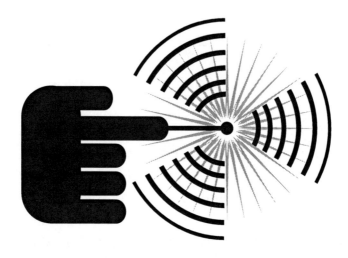

INSANE PRACTICE

It was quiet at the practice track. Most of the racers had already left, but RV was greeted with a nice surprise. He saw his good buddy, Fast Earnie, who was practicing while Madame Insane timed him from the sidelines. Deluxe was thrilled when she saw them. Being with good friends would be comforting after all they had experienced.

They watched Fast Earnie zoom past the finish line and do a spinout as he turned around. When he stopped, he morphed from a vehicle into a person. It was cool to watch. Fast Earnie wiped his brow after his workout. When he heard a familiar voice, he looked up.

"Hey, bro! It's good to see you," said RV as he slapped his friend on the back.

"RV! What are you doing here?" asked Fast Earnie.

"I'm racing in the Majors," said RV.

Fast Earnie was surprised. "No way!" he said. "I thought you weren't into it."

All RV could say was, "It's a long story."

Fast Earnie put his arm around Deluxe's shoulder and said, "It's so great to see you!"

"Looking good, girl!" said Madame Insane as she gave her a hug.

Fast Earnie pointed at Smokescreen and said, "Hey, who's this guy?"

Deluxe smiled. "This is Smokescreen, our new friend."

Fast Earnie shook hands with him. "Hey, Smokescreen. This is my lovely wife, Madame Insane."

"I'm very pleased to meet you, Madame," said Smokescreen, and he kissed her politely on the hand.

Fast Earnie seized the opportunity to boast about his wife. "She's really something. I'll tell ya … if it weren't for her … I'd be … well, look at me. I'm what you call rough around the edges. Hey, do you know how I met my wife?"

RV and Deluxe smiled at each other. This was one of the things that endeared Fast Earnie to them. He loved to tell everyone all about his wife and how they met. Deluxe laughed because she had heard this story so many times.

Fast Earnie pulled his wife close to him as if he was going to dance with her.

"Y-y-yessh!" Madame Insane comically teased him with a twinkle in her eye. She was going to have fun while he told his story

85

"One day I was eating lunch, and this girl came into the DLG Café. Oh, my!" Fast Earnie began.

He twirled Madame Insane and she followed his lead. He recounted how she had been sitting at the table next to his and how he managed to get up the nerve to talk to her. He shared how smitten he was with her beauty and that he was so surprised when she actually fell in love with him.

Smokescreen thought it was peculiar that Madame Insane's clothes changed every time he looked away and looked back at her. Did anyone else see the same thing? It was mystifying. Obviously, they could not all be looking back at her at the same time.

Her outfits were stunning. He looked away. When he looked back, she had changed from a long scaly mermaid skirt to an evening gown with black gloves and a necklace of gems.

Then there was Madame Insane's hair, which actually came to life at times. Strands of hair gathered together and formed what looked like dozens of slithering arms. At one point, one strand grabbed a soda from the cooler while another put a straw in it. She took sips occasionally as Fast Earnie shared his story.

"Isn't she something?" said Fast Earnie as he hugged his wife.

"Oh, yes sir, most definitely," said Smokescreen.

RV and Deluxe laughed. They really enjoyed their friends, but now it was time to get down to business.

RV said, "So is this where we practice?"

"Yeah, man. Go for it," said Fast Earnie.

"I might as well have some fun!" said RV, and he whistled through his flute nose. "Let's go! It's a race!"

He took off around the practice track.

Fast Earnie felt a tug on his arm. It was Smokescreen.

"Excuse me, Mr. Earnie. Is that your cooler over there?"

Smokescreen pointed to a cooler of food that Fast Earnie and Madame Insane had brought with them.

"It sure is. Are you hungry, Smokescreen? Help yourself," said Fast Earnie.

He picked up a pair of scopes and watched RV, fascinated. "He is so fast. Whew! Look at him on that wheel. He doesn't even have a motor and he's faster than any unicycle I've ever seen. He's going to have to race against the full-engine unicycles."

Then he said to Madame Insane, "Baby, give Deluxe the scopes so she can check it out."

Deluxe watched RV race around the track. She'd always known he loved to race, but she never realized how fast he was. She was impressed when she heard Fast Earnie talk about him.

Then she looked through the scopes and was troubled when she saw E-racer on the other side of the track. She decided to keep an eye on him.

E-racer wanted to practice as well. He pointed his formidable index finger from the sidelines and got ready to shoot.

"P-p-practice ... practice ... I-I-I need to practice ... I-I-I need to practice," E-racer said to himself. He shot a bright green ray of laser light from his finger and instantly hit RV's wheel. The wheel disintegrated and RV tumbled to the ground. E-racer gasped, "Uh-oh!"

He knew he would be in trouble with the Major, but still, he laughed wickedly. He thought it looked funny! Sadly, he wasn't concerned about RV at all. He was so used to e-racing creatures and people that this was just another disposable person to him. He couldn't remember anything he had previously e-raced, so this calamity didn't matter much either.

Deluxe lowered the scopes. She had seen everything. All RV's friends ran to where he lay helpless on the ground. He was completely unaware of what had happened.

Deluxe held up his head, wiped his brow with a tissue, and said, "RV! Are you all right?"

"I'm okay. What happened?"

"I saw the whole thing," said Deluxe as she pointed to the offender on the sidelines. "E-racer shot at you with his finger and your wheel disintegrated."

RV looked down at where his wheel used to be and said, "My wheel disappeared! I thought the Major wanted to race against me. How am I supposed to race tomorrow?"

Fast Earnie said, "Let's calm down a minute and think this thing through."

Deluxe saw E-racer laughing and said to her friends, "I'll be right back." She angrily marched over to him.

Now this girl was a very kind aardvark, but she was also so forthright and honest that excuses could never hold up against a rebuke from her. She stood in front of the villain with the treacherous index finger and shouted,

"E-racer! I saw what you did to RV. You should be ashamed of yourself!"

"W-w-well …" E-racer gulped—and that was all that came out of his mouth.

His conscience had been pricked, and he'd actually listened to what Deluxe said. She wasn't finished with him, though. She wanted justice for her friend.

"E-racer!" she repeated with piercing eyes. "You should point that finger at yourself. Maybe then you could e-race all that's bad inside of you!"

She didn't give him a chance to speak. She turned right around and went back to RV.

E-racer was taken aback. He really liked Deluxe, and what she'd said was true. He was really bad—but what had made him that way? Disappointed with himself, he looked down at his finger. Could he really get rid of all that was bad inside? He slowly pointed his powerful index finger at his own heart. If he shot it at himself, would he disappear? It was too late! The green ray entered into his chest.

It hurt. The pain was intense, but he did not disappear. Fortunately for E-racer, his finger had a different effect when he pointed it at himself than when he pointed it at others. Could Deluxe have been right? He was starting to think differently. Something within him had changed.

He looked at RV lying on the field and immediately understood the pain he had caused him. He knew he was responsible for all the wicked schemes he had devised with Major Tomm. It was as if until this moment, E-racer had been oblivious to good and evil, and now the truth was clear to him.

RV sat up. His eyes were fixed on the place where his wheel used to be. He told Fast Earnie and Madame Insane why he had entered the Major Races. How would losing his wheel affect his ability to protect Deluxe? If he did not compete, at the very least, the Major would have him fined or thrown into prison. Then it hit him—he could not move!

"I'm going to need a new wheel," RV said.

The others were cautious in their response. After all, RV was the *blur of blue*. For a very long time, he had been the example to everyone who knew him that anything was possible, but now, without his wheel, he was helpless. Perhaps he should forget about the race. Where could an aardvark get a wheel—let alone, be able to use it right away?

Deluxe was hopeful and said, "What about Proton? He just invented that new wheel."

Smokescreen said, "Proton left early this morning and is probably on the other side of the planet by now."

"I have an idea," said RV. He pulled a small device out of the compartment in his belly and clipped it onto his left wrist. "I have this TV. It's a travel vox. I've never used it before, but I could try it."

They all stared at it curiously.

Fast Earnie finally asked, "What in the world is a travel vox?"

RV explained. "My father invented this gadget, and I promised only to use it in an emergency. A travel vox is for time travel."

"No way," said Fast Earnie. "Does that thing really work?"

"It worked for my father," said RV. "Maybe we could travel back in time to yesterday afternoon. We could catch Proton before he leaves on his trip. Who knows? Maybe I could get one of his new wheels. It's a long shot, but it might work."

"Travel back in time?" Madame Insane exclaimed. She wanted to cheer up everyone. "Happy day! That's so cool. Let's do it."

RV continued to explain and said, "We should be able to travel back to the present once I have the wheel."

"I think we should at least try it," said Deluxe.

The group was in wholehearted agreement.

"There's only one problem," said RV. "You have to be moving at a very high speed in order for time travel to work, but I can't move at all."

"No problem," said Fast Earnie. "I'll be your ride."

He immediately transformed himself into a race vehicle. He let down his convertible top and shouted, "Everybody, hop in!"

The others helped RV into the front seat, and Smokescreen sat at the wheel. Fast Earnie revved the engine.

RV said, "Take us to the intersection of Major City and Gnarly Forest."

Fast Earnie took off and drove full speed ahead. When they entered the intersection, RV pushed the red button on the travel vox, and the vehicle dissolved into thin air.

E-racer was deep in new thoughts as he left the practice track. The intense discomfort from pointing his finger at himself was gone. In fact, he was no longer distressed over anything. He had faced his own shame. For the first time in his life, he had a clean conscience.

He sang as he went back to the fuelsolage garage, "No more. No more e-racing for me!"

E-racer carried armfuls of e-racer gel capsules and dumped them into the bin marked *Trash*.

"Dumping, dumping, dumping," he sang. "No more e-racing for me. From now on, I-I-I'm going to be n-n-nice!"

He stopped for a moment and said aloud in an innocent voice full of determination, "I like nice!"

CHAPTER TWELVE

GIMME A HEAD WITH HAIR

The gang manifested out of thin air at the fork in the road where the two signs stood.

"Woohoo! That was weird!" Madame Insane laughed.

"Is it really yesterday afternoon?" asked Deluxe.

RV read the signs and said, "Look! The signs say Major City and Gnarly Forest."

RV, Smokescreen, and Deluxe had already seen the Gnarly Forest and wanted to avoid it, but what was about to happen would convince them that they really had traveled back in time.

The large tree slowly opened its eyes just as it had done the previous day. Several other trees nearby opened their eyes, and their twisted branches moved like arms. The very large tree opened its mouth wide, and as it let out its bloodcurdling laugh, hundreds of winged creatures flew out into the sky—just as they had done the day before.

"WHOA! I just had a déjà vu," said Smokescreen. "What a strange experience! It's as if I've been here before. Wait a minute, I *have* been here before." Suddenly, the reason he'd had the first déjà vu occurred to him. "Hmm … I wonder if time travel causes déjà vu," he said quietly.

The windert flew past his nose again. The old tree opened its eyes and repeated its angry stare at them. Several giant ratchulas scurried across the ground, and the overgrown spyderoid peaked out from behind a tree.

Full of life, Madame Insane boisterously took the initiative. "Well, kids, it looks like we're going to have to pass through the Gnarly Forest to get to Proton's place."

Smokescreen wanted to avoid the forest and said, "Madame, this forest looks much too dense to drive through."

However, Madame Insane was enthusiastic about taking on the difficult task and said, "No worries. Deluxe, sit up here with me, girl." The two girls sat up high on the back seat together. Then Madame Insane patted her husband and said, "Baby, you know what to do."

Madame's thick beautiful waves of hair flowed gracefully in different directions. Several locks formed mysterious arm-strands just as they had done at the practice track. Dozens of strands moved around—each with a will of its own. Some locks formed into shears.

Fast Earnie drove into the forest just as this metamorphosis occurred, and Madame Insane's hair clipped its way through the dreaded woodland.

Predators flew in the sky, searching for prey. These threatening muggentuts swooped down with great speed and screeched horribly in front of them. One of Madame Insane's strands of hair took the shape of a python and bolted forward. It appeared to have a mouth, and it let out a startling roar like that of a wild beast. The sound resonated with such a vibration that the muggentuts scattered in every direction.

"AGH!" Deluxe screamed.

A giant spyderoid dropped down in front of her face by the thread of its silvery web. One of Madame Insane's strands formed a hair net and captured it while other strands continued to clip away the trees. She disposed of the trapped creature in the net and hung it like an ornament on a branch.

Madame Insane waved to the spyderoid and called in a sassy tone, "BA-BYE, NOW!"

It is difficult to describe all that was going on at the same time, but I will tell you this: Madame Insane's hair conquered the challenges of the Gnarly Forest so adeptly that she and Deluxe could just sit back and enjoy the ride. The two girls not only chitchatted while her hair worked its magic, but they even touched up their make-up.

When a swarm of izabees swirled toward them, a strand shaped itself into a hive that attracted the buzzing creatures, and one got stuck in Deluxe's hair.

"What is that?" asked Deluxe, scratching her head.

Another strand pulled the izabee out by its wings. Madame Insane held the creature out so Deluxe could see it.

"IZ-A-BEE!" she shouted with a hearty laugh. A moment later, hundreds of izabees swarmed to attack her. She roared again and shouted, "IZ-A-BOOO!" The frightened izabees flew away helter skelter.

A strand of Madame's hair took the hive, which was dripping with sweet sticky nectar, and handed it to a Cartesian grizmot standing on the side of the road. Grizmots love sticky nectar, and no grizmot could be happier than this one.

Deluxe exclaimed, "This is insane."

Madame Insane winked at her and laughed. "Happy day!"

Smokescreen had never seen anything like this. He looked at the girls from time to time as they talked and primped, astounded by Madame Insane's powerful hair. And still, every time he looked at her, she changed outfits!

The group finally came to a clearing that looked like the entrance to Proton's place and stepped out of the vehicle. When they turned to look back, they marveled at the path of neatly trimmed trees behind them. Fast Earnie morphed back into a person. What a wild ride!

Smokescreen, in his overly polite manner of speaking, was the first to say something. He was in awe of what had just happened, but he did not know exactly how to compliment Madame Insane on her performance.

"Madame, that is what I call some outstanding tree trimming," was all he could say.

With her hand on her hip and a twinkle in her eye, Madame Insane fluffed her long beautiful hair and said, "That's what you call a good hair day!"

CHAPTER THIRTEEN

PROTON AND THE WHEEL

The friends were exhilarated by what they had just experienced. They had not only traveled back in time and made it through the dreaded Gnarly Forest, but now they looked forward to the possibility of meeting the famous Proton. They all hoped he would be able to help RV. Fast Earnie and Madame Insane had already met the popular athlete at one of the previous Major Races, but they doubted he would remember them.

The gang continued on foot for about half a mile. Fast Earnie carried his injured pal, while the sound of wheels turning could be heard in the distance.

"What is that?" asked Smokescreen.

RV felt a rush of adrenalin.

They moved closer and saw a stone sign that read, "Proton Arena." Nearby, they saw what looked liked a figure doing aerials on a vert ramp.

"There he is," said Fast Earnie in a respectful tone. "It's Proton. Check it out."

Proton had been a role model for both RV and Fast Earnie. The skater had a good reputation, and kids looked up to him because he was cool, decent, and a phenomenal competitor.

They got closer and saw a circular arena in a private stone amphitheater. It was secluded because the Gnarly Forest surrounded it. Proton skated back and forth on the largest ramp that RV and Fast Earnie had ever seen. He was fast and smooth as he sailed on the half-pipe. He glided up the vertical walls, and his laser light wings glowed an electric purple blue. He soared in the air and poised in a unique way with every turn. He maneuvered into unexpected transitions each time he dropped down from an aerial. What great tricks! He seemed to be making them up as he went along. His visitors watched him, mesmerized.

Proton noticed the group as he flew up the vert ramp and landed on the platform. You would think he would have been upset at the sight of uninvited guests in his private skate park, but he smiled and walked toward them.

"Fast Earnie, Madame Insane! How did you find your way back here?" he asked. He remembered them. Then he saw RV in Fast Earnie's arms and said, "Hey, aren't you the Racer Aardvark?"

What a kick! He recognized RV, who acted completely at ease in the presence of his childhood hero, despite having to meet him under such embarrassing circumstances.

RV shook hands and said, "Yes, that would be me. Hello, Proton. I have to say, it is an honor to meet you."

"Hey, man, I've heard a lot about you," said Proton.

It was amazing that they all felt so comfortable and at home.

RV said, "Well, I've heard a lot about you, too! Like, who hasn't?"

Fast Earnie felt that taking care of his buddy was urgent and said, "We really need your help, Proton. Our friend here is supposed to race in the Major Races—"

"—and Major Tomm's assistant, E-racer, disintegrated my wheel," RV blurted out.

Proton's face dropped when he realized that RV had no feet.

Deluxe explained, "We heard about the new wheel you invented, and we were hoping you could help. I'm Deluxe, by the way, and this is Smokescreen."

The famous skater was moved by his visitors' sincere wish to help their friend. He looked at them and said, "Just wait a moment. I'll be right back."

Madame Insane smiled at Fast Earnie. "What a great guy!" she said. "I can't believe he remembered us."

"He was one of my favorite athletes when I was a kid. I can even remember taking Proton vitamins," Fast Earnie replied.

"I remember those vitamins," said Deluxe.

Madame Insane added, "Oh yeah! They came in different colors, didn't they? And they were shaped like Proton doing different tricks."

RV opened the compartment in his belly, pulled out a small container, and said, "What are you guys talking about? *Remember* Proton vitamins? I still take them!"

They busted up laughing as he handed one to each of them. Proton returned with what looked like an oversized suitcase. He cracked up when RV gave him a vitamin.

"I didn't know they still made these," Proton said as he popped the pill into his mouth.

He laid the luggage case on the ground and unzipped it. It was full of wheels in different sizes and a myriad of colors.

"You know, I'm supposed to fly out tomorrow morning to meet with my manufacturer," he said. "I have all these prototypes." He pulled out a new wheel, handed it to RV, and said, "This size looks like it would fit you."

He adjusted the unbelievably fine piece of equipment onto RV's lower body until it fit properly.

RV spun the wheel with his hand and said, "Whoa! This feels good." He'd never had a wheel like it. "Thank you. Thank you so much."

Proton had been very generous, but he also had some concerns.

"I have to warn you. This wheel is ten times more intense than anything you've ever used. You may want to try it out first, because you'll probably need to get used to it," he said.

RV stood up slowly, barely keeping his balance. The wheel was exceptional, but he had to lean on his friends to keep from falling over. Deluxe walked with him for a while and let him hold onto her arm.

RV looked at Proton and asked, "Can I practice on your ramp?"

"Of course," said Proton, "but you've got to check this out first."

He led everyone to the seating section in front of the ramp. RV struggled to keep up with the group.

When they reached the amphitheater, Proton said, "Watch this," as he pushed a remote control.

Ah! Will the wonders of Zein never cease? Proton's amphitheater worked like a carousel.

"We're moving," said Deluxe.

"Yes, we are. This arena has four seating stations that rotate around the show area," Proton explained. "This is the optimum for contests, and especially demos."

The setup allowed an audience to view the different park sections and skating demonstrations. There were also two street-style areas that rotated within themselves; when a skater did tricks, the street equipment turned randomly. Athletes really had to be spontaneous to perform well in this arena. It was awesome!

"Is that a transparent clover bowl?" asked RV.

Proton proudly continued to explain, "This arena allows the audience to see some of the most sophisticated transfers in the history of riding. To answer your question, yes, that *is* a transparent clover bowl in the center of the

PROTON ARENA

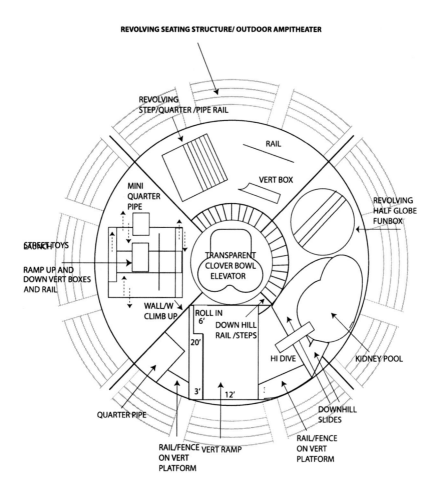

REVOLVING SEATING STRUCTURE/ OUTDOOR AMPITHEATER

REVOLVING
STEP/QUARTER /PIPE RAIL

RAIL

VERT BOX

MINI
QUARTER
PIPE

REVOLVING
HALF GLOBE
FUNBOX

STREET TOYS

TRANSPARENT
CLOVER BOWL
ELEVATOR

RAMP UP AND
DOWN VERT BOXES
AND RAIL

WALL/W
CLIMB UP

ROLL IN
6'

DOWN HILL
RAIL /STEPS

20'

HI DIVE

KIDNEY POOL

3'   12'

QUARTER PIPE

DOWNHILL
SLIDES

RAIL/FENCE
ON VERT
PLATFORM

VERT RAMP

RAIL/FENCE
ON VERT
PLATFORM

arena there. Not only can you see the riders through it, but it also works like an elevator. It's the ultimate spectator experience! RV, would you like to try it?"

"Are you kidding?" RV said. This was unreal! He wanted to jump out of his skin, but his enthusiasm was greater than his ability. He wobbled over to the site and said, "I can't wait! Do you guys mind?"

"No, of course not. Go for it," said the gang—but they all wondered if he could stand up on his own.

"Let me check the TV for a second," said RV as he inspected the time travel vox. "I want to make sure this thing doesn't get damaged."

Once the TV was secured, he joined Proton on the ramp platform … but he hesitated to drop in. He didn't trust his own ability.

Proton initiated and RV followed. They synchronized with one another by doing crossovers. The gang stomped and hooted. Deluxe was completely engrossed, and Smokescreen oohed and aahed while munching on snacks.

Fast Earnie yelled, "You guys are ripping!"

Every once in a while, RV jokingly whistled through his flute nose, but he was actually having a hard time. His lack of balance on the unfamiliar wheel caused radical affects.

RV did double twists on his verts and tricks high in the air that he'd never imagined he could do. He undertook a double-loop high out and spontaneously performed unusual maneuvers. He completed a double axis twist with a 180-degree rollover turn as if he was in the clouds, and then glided down into the half-pipe. It was so cool to watch—until everyone realized that he was totally out of control!

The carousel revolved. Proton climbed onto what looked like a high dive and dropped into the kidney pool. He was completely unaware of RV's predicament.

Deluxe gasped. She could see RV perspiring as he flew onto the stair rail. He bravely whistled through his flute nose and grinded his way down, but he couldn't stop.

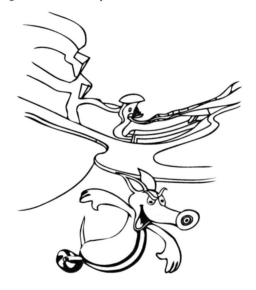

Proton was in another section of the show area where he grinded down the middle of a revolving half-globe. He flipped the deck and caught it as he jumped onto the street section and headed toward the revolving quarter-pipe. When he came out of his trick, he saw RV swoop into the transparent clover bowl. The feat looked sensational, but something was very wrong. When the bowl had completely elevated, RV soared out and over the ramp platform. He whizzed down the center slide towards the kidney pool—and crashed!

"No!" Deluxe screamed.

The sweet little aardvark waitress from the DLG ran to the rescue. Proton also jumped into the pool to see what had happened and saw Deluxe's concern.

He said to RV, "She looks worried. You *were* of out of control."

RV pulled himself up just as Deluxe reached him.

"It's okay," said RV. He tried to laugh it off. He enjoyed getting her attention. "I'm okay. This was fun!"

"Really? Are you sure?" asked Deluxe.

RV hugged her and said, "Yeah!"

He could balance a little bit better after practicing, but his ability to race was debatable.

Proton was troubled by this and asked, "Are you going to be all right? You're not very steady."

"I'll make it in the race," said RV.

"I think you should take a spare with you just in case," said Proton as he fished around in his oversized suitcase and handed him an extra wheel.

"I can't begin to thank you, Proton," said RV.

He tucked the extra wheel into his compartment, and the famous athlete escorted his guests to the amphitheater entrance.

"I have to head out now," Proton said. "I'll see you guys at the Major Races. I'll be doing a demo there."

They thanked him for his hospitality and left. A few moments later, he unexpectedly called out from a distance, "Hey, RV! Give 'em a show at the races!"

"Thanks. I'll remember that!" said RV.

Fast Earnie morphed himself, and the group climbed into the race vehicle.

RV said thoughtfully, "Listen, we have to travel back to the present now, but I want to drop Deluxe off at the DLG before we return to Major City."

When Deluxe heard this, she was surprised and disappointed.

"What? Why?" she said.

RV explained, "Look, I don't know what will take place at the races, and I don't want anything to happen to you."

Madame Insane said, "He wants you to be safe, girl." She explained to Deluxe why RV was concerned. "Who knows what Major Tomm will do? I mean, he did have you kidnapped. Remember?"

"Yeah," said Deluxe. She was disappointed, but she knew RV was right.

Madame Insane encouraged her. "You can watch the races on the big screen at the DLG, and we'll all come by the restaurant afterward."

"Well, okay," said Deluxe with a sigh.

Now, all in agreement, they sped off and disappeared into time travel.

CHAPTER FOURTEEN

LET THE GAMES BEGIN

The three suns had risen over the rolling hills of Major City, and the sounds from the Major Races Event could be heard in the distance.

"This is so beautiful," said Madame Insane.

Fast Earnie's eyes sparkled with amusement as he leaned in close to his wife. "Yes, you are," he said.

She blushed as he lightly brushed his hand against her cheek. He always let her know how special she was to him. It was one of the things she liked about being married.

At the entry arch, RV saw a large sign that read, "12th Annual Major Races and Sporting Event." A voice welcomed the visitors and athletes over the loudspeaker. The gang was excited as they entered the gate. They saw a spectacular hubbub of diverse species gathered together: aardvarks and mobilots, humatozoids, teldistars, man-droinots, woman-droinots, kids and babies, and moms and dads. There were sideshows and concession stands, races and contests, musicians and bake-ticians, dancing and food. Everywhere you looked there was something cool to do, and folks were having fun.

The smell of freshly baked goods filled the air. A bunch of kids jumped up and down on a giant inflatable pieod. There were also pieod wrestlers and pieod concession stands, and one fellow was pushing an ice pieod cart around the park. Many competitions were featured simultaneously at the Major Races, and athletes gave autographs between events.

RV and Fast Earnie wanted to see the Psyche-X Contest; the gang followed along out of curiosity. They reached the top of the arena just in time to see one of the riders cycle down the ramp. Psyche-X was a double-wheeled sport, and the riders had to be highly aggressive to overcome unique obstacles. The rider descended the ramp toward the first obstacle, picking up speed. He launched into the air and did a double bar spin. Then he rode down again, picking up speed, and launched off the next obstacle. He did another bar spin in mid-air, making a 360-degree overhead flip at the same time. Then he flew over the launch to the other side.

RV and Fast Earnie applauded the rider, and the entire audience cheered.

The announcer shouted, "It's J-Dog Delray! This guy is psyched!"

Another announcer quickly added, "Oh yeah, psyched with skill!"

J-Dog Delray climbed upside the next launch and came out of a 360.

The sportscaster yelled, "Look at this. He's come down from his aerial and launched off his next obstacle with even more power. He's high in the air. He's flipped overhead once, twice … Ho! A full 720!"

An overpass had been built for guests who wanted to go from one event to another. RV, Fast Earnie, Madame Insane, and Smokescreen crossed it to watch the rounders prepare for their race. Rounders were small, one-man vehicles that rode close to the ground. They had four large ball-shaped wheels with heavily grooved treads. They could travel on any terrain and move in any direction—forward, backward, and sideways.

The start bell rang. The rounders sped toward the viewers, kicking up dust on the bare grunge track. The lead racer wove in and out, passing his opponents as he accelerated.

"Check out number seven," said the broadcaster. "He's way ahead! It's Showtime Rasta!"

Showtime Rasta was famous for being what you call random. He loved to perform, and that is why he got the nickname *Showtime*.

Out of the blue, Showtime lifted himself up onto the handlebars and did a handstand. He apparently enjoyed taking the lead in this race, and of course, he had to do something random.

The announcer was stunned. "What's this?" he said. "A handstand—? Wait! A flag just popped out of Showtime's shoe! It says 'Hi Mom!' Hah! That's Showtime for ya! Woo hoo!"

RV and the gang moved to the next event and heard one of the sportscasters say, "We're here with the monstrols!"

The creatures wore rollers that looked like shoes with one large wheel. A reptilian monster droid stepped out to do his heat, and the announcer yelled, "It's Iggy-Boy Droid."

Iggy-Boy Droid's rollers had rockets in back of them, and they fired up. He rode down the ramp where he caught huge air, lifted off the edge, and did a 1080-degree overhead spin.

"Triple Overhead!"

Iggy came out of his aerial and smoothly glided back down the ramp.

He landed on one foot with his one-wheeled skate and came to a full stop. The announcer said, "One-skate landing with a full stop! Ho! That's history, boys."

A lot of kids had seen RV and Fast Earnie. They surrounded them and asked for their autographs.

Fast Earnie signed one and said, "RV! Look at that over there."

A group of kids dressed up as monstrols skated by them. These kids were obviously humatozoids dressed up for fun. Each wore a helmet that looked like the head of a monstrol, except for the youngest one. The little guy in the group wore a homemade helmet that looked just like RV's head.

Fast Earnie said, "Hey, that little guy looks like you."

RV was amused along with his friends and had to admit that it *was* funny.

Then they heard over the loudspeaker, "Fastrak Racers, prepare for your event. Fastrak Racers, prepare for your event!"

Madame Insane kissed Fast Earnie on the cheek and said, "That's you, baby. I'll be rooting for you!"

Madame Insane noticed the look on RV's face. She knew he closely watched her and her husband. She also knew that RV loved Deluxe.

"I know you're missing Deluxe, RV," Madame Insane said to him gently. "It'll be all right."

RV looked up at her with puppy dog eyes, grateful for her insight.

Then he felt an unexpected tug on his arm. It was the little monstrol with the RV helmet. He looked at the boy's face under the helmet and recognized him as the fourteen-month-old from the DLG. He was still sucking on his pacifier.

RV was surprised and said, "I remember you."

The little guy held out a paper and pen.

"You want my autograph? Sure! Wow, I didn't think you were old enough to walk," said RV.

A girl who was also dressed as a monstrol spoke up. "He can't. That's my little brother. He can't walk, but he can roll!"

RV looked down at his own wheel and smiled, "Hey, he really is like me!"

CHAPTER FIFTEEN

THINGS THAT
GO FAST

The customers at the DLG Café had gathered around the big screen with anticipation.

Two famous on-screen announcers, Casper and Blowtorch, stood in front of a blinking logo and proclaimed, "Welcome to Eccentric Racing Network!"

A young humatozoid named Kenia was watching with her girlfriends. Since they knew many of the guys who came to the café to watch the races, the event was all the more fun.

The on-screen image changed to the Major Races and Sporting Event, and the scene settled on the Fastrak.

Kenia turned around excitedly and announced, "The Fastrak races are up next."

Dee, the owner of the DLG, told Deluxe that Fast Earnie's race was starting. Deluxe moved closer to the screen to get a better view, but it went static.

"What's wrong with the picture?" said Dee. The viewers at the café booed with disappointment

A moment later, the picture returned. The race had begun, and everyone cheered! Several racers were ahead of Fast Earnie when he made his first turn. Then they formed a single line in the far right lane. The vehicles moved so quickly that it was difficult to follow them on the screen.

Fast Earnie did a 360-degree skid, but he quickly got back into the race. He passed two of the vehicles and one of the racers lost control. The viewers watched as the vehicle lost its way and rolled off the track.

"Oh, no!" said Kenia.

Everyone was relieved that the driver had survived the crash. He started back up, but he did not get back into the race. The girls commented to each other about the accident.

"I'll be right back," said Deluxe, her brow creased with worry.

She hurried to the back of the café, pushed through the stock room doors, leaned against the wall, and prayed. "Please don't let anything happen to RV when he races. Protect him from Major Tomm. He's my best friend, and I love him." She took a deep breath as if she had been surprised by a revelation and said, "I … love … him."

She could not believe the words had come out of her mouth, yet she could not deny it was true.

Back at the races, Fast Earnie was on the Fastrak. He whirred around a curve and onto the straightaway. In a matter of seconds, he was in the lead.

Casper, one of the sportscasters, shouted at the top of his lungs, "The white flag goes up for Fast Earnie. Let's see … Will he make it to the victory lane?"

Fast Earnie accelerated as he came out of the straightaway. He rounded the last curve, and no other racer was even close. The checkered flag went down.

Blowtorch, the other announcer, roared, "There are plenty of fans here for Fast Earnie! They are jumping up and down as Fast Earnie wins the 12th Annual Fastrak Division of the Major Races!"

Madame Insane ran to greet him. Her hair strands popped open celebratory bottles of soda and sprayed them every which way. RV popped open a bottle and sprayed it at Fast Earnie. The crowd cheered. Fast Earnie kissed Madame Insane, and they all gave each other a high five, hugging, hooting, and hollering all at the same time. Fast Earnie popped open another bottle and sprayed his friends.

"Happy day!" shouted Madame Insane.

RV jumped on a bench, cupped his hand to his ear, and egged on the crowd. "Hey! I can't hear you!"

The crowd screamed louder.

Fast Earnie grabbed him and said, "Hey buddy, you're up next."

RV was having too much fun. "I know. I know," he said.

Smokescreen perked up when he heard this news. Many things could have been said about this metallic droid, but one thing was certain: he was loyal to RV.

"Excuse me, everyone. I am going to the snack bar, and I will return shortly," he said.

Fast Earnie mused as he watched him walk away. "Have you ever noticed? That dude's always eating."

Madame Insane had a craving for some treats and ran after Smokescreen. "Can you get me an ice pieod from the snack bar?" she asked.

Smokescreen looked serious and said, "Madame, I must tell you that I am not actually going to the snack bar. I am going to keep an eye on E-racer so he doesn't harm Sir RV during the race."

Smokescreen's statement warmed her heart. She was surprised that he was so willing to look out for his friend.

Madame Insane smiled, patted him on the back, and said, "Wow, Smokescreen! Good man!"

If RV's race was up next, then so was Major Tomm's. The Major was more than prepared, not only to race, but to receive the trophy and all the glory that followed. He was dressed in a bright new uniform, a shiny new helmet, and brand new boots. He could not find E-racer anywhere, but the oddity-bots were available to cater to his every whim.

Major Tomm entered the fuelsolage garage. He popped open the back of the Uni-Racer 5000 to install its fuel capsules and turned to the oddity-bot behind him.

"Two-Two, install this fuel," he commanded.

"Yes sir!" the droid responded with clinking robotic noises as he lifted capsules from the trash bin.

Two-Two did not realize that he was loading the e-racer gel capsules that E-racer thought he had thrown out.

"Unicycle racers, prepare for your event," said the announcer. "Unicycle racers, prepare for your event!"

Major Tomm was busy thinking about the race, but he was bothered by E-racer's absence. He tried to contact him on his pocket vu-screen communicator.

"E-RACER!" yelled the Major.

No one knew about E-racer's change of heart. The stuttering assistant was avoiding his boss on purpose.

"I don't have time for this right now," said the Major. "Two-Two, I've got to get out to the Fastrak right away. I need you to find E-racer and have him call me on my vu-screen. He's supposed to e-race the aardvark's wheel bolt during the race. Take care of that for me."

"Yes sir," said the oddity-bot as he finished loading the fuel capsules.

Major Tomm saw the fuel door shut and asked, "Are you sure all the fuel is loaded?"

Two-Two said, "Yes sir." (It seemed the only thing Two-Two was capable of saying was, "Yes sir.")

Major Tomm climbed into the Uni-Racer 5000. This was the moment he had been eagerly awaiting.

"All right, then," said the Major as he closed the hatch.

He revved the engine, the garage door opened, and the vehicle rolled out. The fuelsolage garage door started to close, and Two-Two noticed the uni-racer fuel sign lying on the ground. He picked it up and threw it in the bin marked *Trash*.

CHAPTER SIXTEEN

WHICH WAY DID HE GO?

Dee was busily working behind the counter at the DLG Café when she looked up at the screen.

"Deluxe!" she called. "RV's race! Get over here. He's up next."

Kenia and her friends yelled, "There he is! There's RV!"

The unicycle racers lined up for their event, and the girls caught a good look at RV.

Torley jumped up and said, "He's so cute!"

Kenia said, "He really is. I heard he's nice too!"

Cushy asked, "Doesn't he come in here sometimes?"

Deluxe stood behind the counter, listening to them. RV had been her best friend for a long time, but suddenly, when the other girls showed an interest in him, she felt insecure.

"Deluxe knows him," said Kenia.

The whole group turned toward Deluxe, hoping that she might help them meet RV.

"Really?" Cushy asked, "Do you think you could introduce us sometime?"

Deluxe only hoped that her face did not reveal her thoughts.

"Sure," she said. "He's my best friend."

The girls were thrilled.

Little Cushy, who was very interested in RV, said, "Thanks, Deluxe. That would be so cool!"

Torley pointed at the big screen and said, "Hey! Look at those crazy unicycle racers!"

The unicycles were lined up at the start line, and the girls commented on each one. Number eight looked like an eight ball. In fact, the vehicle's wheel was not a wheel at all, but a ball. It was like a rounder in that it allowed the racer to move backward, forward, and from side to side very easily. The driver climbed inside and quickly closed the top hatch. They could see him through the window, which had the number eight painted on it. The girls giggled.

"He's an eight ball. Ha ha ha!" said Kenia.

Torley chimed in, "Wait! No. Look at this next one!"

Racer number fifteen looked like a robotic ducky with a pinwheel hat.

"He's a ducky-wucky. Maybe he'll be a wucky-ducky!" Torley said.

Without warning, their ducky-wucky hiccupped, and the vehicle rose several feet into the air! As he came down, his pinwheel hat spun around.

"Aw, he must be nervous," said Cushy.

Racer number zero, or Oh Boy, as he was called, was up next. Oh Boy's vehicle looked like a giant inner tube. The racer held onto a handle bar that emitted jet fire on each side. When the inner tube moved, the jets propelled it forward.

Kenia was flabbergasted and said, "No way! An inner tube? Well, I guess it *is* one wheel."

Oh Boy had a curious reputation on Zein. Every person on the planet had spoken his name aloud at some time in his or her life. It was common to hear things like "Oh Boy! This tastes great" or "Oh Boy! We're going to have fun today." The strange thing was that no one seemed to know who Oh Boy was. He was not only a real person, but he was also very important. His family grew the plants that purified the droxiden on Zein; people could not survive without clean droxiden to drink.

The spectators could see number seven in the line-up, who was none other than RV, the Racer Aardvark.

"There's RV!" said Cushy. "He's so cute."

Then they saw the Uni-Racer 5000 next to RV.

"And there's Major Tomm!" said Torley.

The announcers proclaimed, "Ladies and Gentlemen, the Major Races and Sporting Event presents the Unicycle

Races. This is the event we have all been waiting to see. Unies, prepare to start your race!"

The viewers could see the other racers in the event. There was number thirty-one, who was a skinny dude driver with a cubed head. He drove an electric unicycle. This vehicle's giant battery charged as its wheel turned. There was also racer number forty-four, whose vehicle looked like a space car. Number twenty-two had a giant jet-propelled wheel. Number sixty-four was a purple racer who looked like a penguin with a headset.

RV prepared for his race. He had become more comfortable with his new wheel, but he was still apprehensive as to how well he would be able to control it in the race. He looked up into the crowd and saw Madame Insane and Fast Earnie waving at him. They were his only friends in the stands. He looked around and wondered, *What happened to Smokescreen?* He was nowhere in sight.

The start lights lit up. The flag went down and a gun went off. The race had begun. RV moved awkwardly. He wasn't balancing very well on Proton's wheel, and he lacked speed.

Oh Boy, the inner tube, sped ahead. He held the handlebars fast as the jets fired on each side. He was making good time. The eight ball moved backward, forward, and from side to side around each racer, but then he got stuck behind the ducky-wucky. The ducky-wucky hiccupped, and it sent him several feet off the ground again. The eight ball moved ahead and rolled right underneath him. The ducky-wucky spun on his pinwheel until he hit the ground and continued to race.

RV whistled through his flute nose, "Let's go! It's a race!"

He sounded enthusiastic as he entered the mix, but he was well aware that his wheel skills were questionable. Still, he had made a promise to Proton that he would make it in the race. He sped ahead with his eye on the eight ball, but its driver maneuvered so well that RV could not get around it.

Major Tomm was racing in the Uni-Racer 5000, which was definitely the most impressive looking vehicle on the track. He sang to himself from inside his vehicle and confidently assumed he owned this race.

"Me, me, me, me! I'm so in love with *me!*" Major Tomm sang as he looked down at his speedometer. "Everybody watch me!

Number thirty-one, the skinny dude on the electric unicycle, was just ahead of him. "I think my neighbor needs to borrow my battery cables," said the Major with a nasty laugh. He passed the racer. Then he stuck his head out the window and held out giant battery cables. With a dirty look on his face, he said, "Looking for these?"

Number thirty-one was surprised to see Major Tomm. Somehow the Major whipped the giant battery cables out the window and managed to get them in contact with Thirty-one's openly exposed battery. Sparks flew everywhere. Thirty-one was electrocuted!

"AAAGHH!" cried Thirty-one as he fell off his cycle.

"One down," the Major sang to himself.

RV remained unsuccessful at getting around the eight ball. When he tried to move to the left, the driver rode in front of him. If he tried to move to the right, number eight would beat him to it. The Racer Aardvark couldn't seem to pick up speed for the life of him.

Meanwhile, Smokescreen was busy working on his plan. He had decided that he would find E-racer in order to keep an eye on him. Then he would distract the green culprit so that he would not be able to harm RV during the race. Bless his heart—Smokescreen did not know that the Major's menacing assistant had changed. E-racer no longer had any intention of harming anyone. In fact, he would never help the Major again.

Smokescreen, who liked to think of himself as a master of disguise, dressed himself up as an ice pieod vender. Wearing a white cloak, a beanie, and a fake mustache, he approached the booths where the guests placed bets on the competitions. He was enjoying this. He even took on a fake accent. It was an obvious fake, but Smokescreen didn't realize this.

He pushed the ice pieod cart along and shouted, "Ice pieod! Getta you ice pieod. Getta you skishy-skooshy, oh, so juicy, tootsie-vrootsie ice pieod!"

"Five dramacas on number seven," E-racer said to the booth attendant.

Smokescreen rolled his cart as close to E-racer as he could.

"Hey, guy! I gotta sometin' hot for you," Smokescreen said.

Ice pieod *was* E-racer's favorite treat, but right now he was annoyed with this vender. He was trying to place a bet, and this guy was bugging him.

"N-n-no thanks. I-I-I just ate!" said E-racer. "Besides, I-I-I don't like h-h-hot ice pieod."

"Oh, come-a over here!" Smokescreen would not give up. He continued in a secretive half whisper. "I no sell no ice pieod. That's-a phony baloney. I gotta tips on the races. I gotta sometin' you can't-a lose! One dramaca."

E-racer felt like this guy was getting really pushy. "N-n-no, s-s-sorry," he said. "Some other time. I-I-I'm betting on the a-a-aardvark."

Smokescreen paused for a moment because he was confused. *Why would E-racer bet on the aardvark?*

He forgot his fake accent in his surprise and said, "You? You are betting on the aardvark?"

E-racer said, "Y-y-yes. Hey! W-w-what happened to your accent?"

Smokescreen was caught! He was not quite sure what to say. He did not trust E-racer so he continued to stick with his original plan. He used his fake accent again.

"NO. NO. NO. NO! You no wanna bet on no aardvark! He's the worst one-a on the track."

E-racer protested, "Th-th-that's not w-w-what I heard."

Smokescreen said, "Aw, just because he's the fastest."

Did he just say that? Why did he say that?

E-racer looked at him oddly and said, "Fastest? F-F-Fastest is good." Then he turned to the booth attendant and said, "F-F-Five dramacas on the aardvark p-p-please."

Meanwhile, Major Tomm happily steered the Uni-Racer 5000 toward his goal. He looked in front of him and saw Oh Boy, the inner tube. The Major had a box of tacks in one hand and a dastardly look on his face.

"I'm thinking … flat tire!" Major Tomm laughed.

The Uni-Racer 5000 sped past the inner tube, and the Major dropped tacks out of his window. They hit the inner tube, and it whirred out of control like a deflated balloon. The driver held onto the jet-propelled handlebars for dear life.

RV rode alongside the derailed racer and yelled to him, "Let go!"

Oh Boy let go—only to tumble and crash.

Casper, the announcer said, "Oh no, folks! It looks like we have another injured driver. It's Oh Boy!"

"Oh Boy? That name sounds familiar," Blowtorch remarked inquisitively.

Casper laughed, "Yeah, he's Oh Boy—one of the famous 'Oh' brothers."

RV stopped to help the injured driver.

Blowtorch blasted, "And what's this? RV, the Racer Aardvark has stopped to help? Will he be eliminated for helping a fellow racer?"

The sound of the alarm was heard as a medical hovercraft called a medhub lowered itself onto the racetrack. This emergency vehicle, shaped like a giant bullet, was able to levitate up and down and from side to side. Its flat bottom allowed it to land on any surface—sand or concrete, mud, or even water.

Casper announced, "Here comes the medhub! It looks like RV can get back into the race. What's this? RV is climbing into the medhub with the injured number zero! What is going on?"

A medical assistant looked at Oh Boy's injuries. The vehicle lifted off the ground and flew to the nearest medical center.

Oh Boy looked up at RV and said, "Thank you."

He was busted up pretty badly. The medical assistant checked his vital signs and pulled RV aside.

"Sir, you have saved this racer's life," said the assistant. "His ribs and his left leg are broken, and his wrists are badly sprained, but he's going to make it."

RV looked at Oh Boy reassuringly and said, "Did you hear that? You're going to be okay."

"You're … my … friend," said the injured racer in a broken voice.

RV smiled compassionately, patted Oh Boy on the arm, and walked to the pilot's window. The medhub was so high in the sky that it was easy to observe the entire grounds of the Major Races. He saw the Uni-Racer 5000, with the ducky-wucky not far behind. The Uni-Racer 5000 blew smoke from its exhaust pipe, and the ducky-wucky broke out coughing and choking.

"Do you have a toolbox?" RV asked the pilot.

"Sure. It's right over there behind the medvar sets," the pilot said.

RV pulled off his new wheel and began to examine it. He twisted a skeg-knife around in it, put it back on, and tightened it with a fodder pen. Then he pulled a small can from his belly compartment and placed several drops of oiner around the perimeter of the wheel bolts.

"I've got to get back in that race," RV said. Below them was a perfect view of Proton as he did vert demos on a massive skate ramp. RV pointed to it. "There! Drop me into Proton's vert ramp."

The surprised pilot said, "From way up here?"

"Yep. Let's do it!" RV said confidently.

The crowd cheered uncontrollably when they saw the racer aardvark dramatically drop from the sky onto the skate ramp. They thought he had been disqualified. Oohs and aahs could be heard as Proton and RV synchronized into double crossovers. They high-fived each other on their last crossover and landed on the top of the ramp platform.

"That was awesome!" said Proton. "But I thought your race was going on right now."

"It is," said RV. "But, hey, you told me to give 'em a show! Do you think you could drop me back into *my* race?"

"Let's do it!" said Proton.

He picked RV up by the back of the neck, flew above the Fastrak with the aardvark in his talons, and dropped him right onto the spot where he had left off. Proton loved it!

Blowtorch blared, "What's this? Proton just dropped number seven, RV, the Racer Aardvark, back into the race. Now, that's a first!"

His fellow announcer explained, "The rules say that you can get back into the race as long as you start where you left off, but RV has a lot of catching up to do. He's missed a couple of laps."

Suddenly the *blur of blue* kicked in and started to pass everyone. Once again, he had his eye on the eight ball. This time, when the driver maneuvered to keep from being passed, RV came up from behind, drove right over him, and sped ahead.

Blowtorch shouted, "Whoa … Look at him go!"

Major Tomm continued to gloat as he sped along in his Uni-Racer 5000.

"Looks like it's going to be winner time for me!" the Major sang presumptuously as he pulled through a curve. "You see, it's all about me! Me, me, me … It's all about me. I am better than everyone else!"

Then out of nowhere, RV passed him. "NOOO! NOOO! NOOO!" cried Major Tomm as he pounded the steering wheel. RV needed to catch up by a couple of laps, but still the Major freaked out. He pulled out his pocket vu-screen and called, "E-RACER! TWO-TWO! It's time! It's time to e-race the aardvark's wheel bolt! Come in! COME IN! EEE-RAAACERRR!"

E-racer had just finished placing his bet, and Smokescreen was happily opening the lid to the ice pieod cart. He pulled out three treats with one hand.

"Hmmm … ice pieod. Oh, so juicy!" said Smokescreen, beaming. He looked into the cart again and pulled out a gigantic rainbow ice pieod. The grin on his face grew even bigger, and his voice got louder with enthusiasm. "Hmmm … BIG ice pieod!"

E-racer walked up behind him.

"I-I-I thought you said th-th-the ice pieod was ph-ph-phony baloney."

Smokescreen was startled, and he turned around to face him. The gigantic ice pieod flew through the air, hit E-racer, and covered him with vroot stains.

"I'm-a so sorry," said Smokescreen as he began to wipe him off. He tried hard not to laugh. "Let-a me clean-a you up."

E-racer tried to push Smokescreen off. He was desperate to get away.

"Th-th-that's okay. N-n-never, never mind. I-I-I'll use the restroom," E-racer said wearily.

Smokescreen said, "That's a good idea. You go ahead and use-a the restroom."

E-racer quickly walked off and found the nearest facility. To his amazement, Smokescreen followed him and made a very loud public announcement.

"GETTA SOME REST WHILE YOU'RE IN THERE!" Smokescreen yelled. "You look-a like you could use a rest! You need-a to take a good rest. Take-a you time."

"G-G-Geez," said E-racer, feeling frustrated and puzzled.

Smokescreen ran and stood against the door. He looked back and forth as he guarded the restroom.

"Yeah, that's it! Take-a you time." He whispered to himself, "I'm-a gonna make sure he gives that e-racer finger a rest. That's what kind-a rest I'm-a talkin' about."

RV had come way up from behind in the race. He had not only made up for his lost laps, but he'd passed every single racer—except one.

"Unbelievable!" said Casper. "RV, the Racer Aardvark, has come from way behind, and he's just passed Major Tomm."

Blowtorch said, "The Major certainly isn't going to like this."

RV gained ground and moved further ahead.

Casper said, "Look at that. RV is leaving Major Tomm in the dust!"

RV sped ahead. He crossed the finish line first, and the crowd roared.

Then the strangest thing happened: Major Tomm disappeared into thin air! The audience gasped.

"What's this?" said Blowtorch. "What happened? Major Tomm has disappeared!"

His announcer buddy said, "Wow! What's up with him? I guess Major Tomm doesn't wanna be a major loser, eh? Talk about not being able to show your face!"

CHAPTER SEVENTEEN

THE PRIZE

In twelve years, no one had ever beaten Major Tomm at one of his own Major Races. RV had caught up from so far behind, and his drop-in with Proton was historical. He received his trophy, and the crowd went wild.

Many in the crowd, however, wondered what had happened to Major Tomm. Several spectators had previously experienced this strange type of disappearance in their own lives. Pets, keys, and clothing (especially socks) had vanished, but for reasons yet unknown.

Was Major Tomm gone for good? It was a very strange way to finish a very strange race.

RV had won first place, and Madame Insane and Fast Earnie were there to celebrate with him. They popped open bottles of soda and sprayed each other. RV looked at his trophy and the cheering crowds, but in all the excitement, there was something missing. E-racer came and shook his hand. That was a nice surprise! Smokescreen, still in disguise, walked up to congratulate him. Yet, in the midst of all this fame and celebration, RV still had a bit of the blues.

Madame Insane glanced at him and said to Fast Earnie, "He's missing Deluxe."

She wanted to encourage him. When good friends know how you're feeling, it's wonderful—especially when *you* don't even know how you're feeling.

"Do you think RV loves Deluxe?" said Fast Earnie. He was completely clueless.

Madame Insane said, "Think? Of course, he loves Deluxe, and Deluxe loves him."

RV overheard Madame Insane's comments. He looked at her with doubtful eyes, but he was hopeful at the same time.

"I heard what you said, and you're right … about Deluxe. I really do love her," said RV. "But how can you say she loves me? She just thinks of me as a friend."

Madame Insane crossed her arms, looked RV in the eye, and said, "You're going to have to trust me on this. Women know women, and I know that girl loves you."

RV was surprised to hear this.

"Really?" he asked. He wanted to be convinced.

"Oh yes. She loves you," said Madame Insane.

Fast Earnie was proud of his wife for being kind to their friend, but something else was on his mind.

"Hey, whatever happened to Major Tomm?" he said. "He disappeared at the end of the race—right into thin air!"

Everyone looked at E-racer. He held an ice pieod that he had finally bought from the vender, and he was still covered with vroot stains.

"UH-OH!" E-racer said awkwardly. He imagined that everyone thought he was the cause of Major Tomm's disappearance.

RV asked him outright, "E-racer, did you e-race Major Tomm?"

"There's no-a way-a!" said Smokescreen in his fake accent. Suddenly, he realized how he sounded and began to speak normally. "I mean that it is simply not possible. Sir, I was keeping an eye on E-racer during the entire race."

"Y-y-you were?" said E-racer. He was confused.

Madame Insane ripped off Smokescreen's mustache.

"What are you doing with this fake mustache?" she said.

"Probably trying to eat it!" said Fast Earnie.

Smokescreen responded in a serious voice. "No sir. I disguised myself. I was keeping E-racer busy during the race so that he would do no harm to Sir RV."

RV was genuinely touched. These were the things that really mattered in life. He had such good friends! He got a little sentimental, and of course, the possibility that Deluxe might be in love with him made everything even sweeter.

Little E-racer stood up to defend himself. "Y-y-you didn't have to do that. Y-y-you s-s-see, Miss Deluxe, well, she scolded me and …"

E-racer proceeded to tell them the whole story of how Deluxe had corrected him. He explained how his thinking had radically changed after he had pointed his finger at himself. He also shared how he trashed all his e-racer gel capsules in the fuelsolage garage.

Then everyone wondered what did happen to Major Tomm. It was a mystery, but E-racer's disintegrating power was the only explanation for what might have happened. RV suggested that they retrace E-racer's steps in the fuelsolage garage.

They made their way back there to investigate. RV looked in the trash bin and pulled out the sign that said, *Uni-Racer Fuel Capsules.* He read it aloud.

RV asked E-racer, "Is this the trash bin where you threw away your gel capsules?"

"Y-y-yes," said E-racer.

RV said, "Well, somehow Major Tomm got e-raced. Could he have mistakenly loaded your discarded gel capsules into his fuel tank?"

E-racer said, "I-I-I think so. Y-y-yes … probably."

RV's face was filled with concern. "Well, if he's e-raced, then where did he go?"

E-racer shrugged his shoulders and said, "I dunno." He rolled his eyes up to the ceiling. "W-w-where everything else goes that gets e-raced, I-I-I guess."

⊙ ⊙ ⊙

☉ RV, the Racer Āardvark ☉

In a place not in space,
In a place outside time,
In a place where the e-raced
Live outside of Zein,
Major Tomm still exists.

Darkness was everywhere. It was a colorless reality where, inside the Uni-Racer 5000, Major Tomm had not yet realized his fate. He seemed to be in outer space, but it was not outer space. This was the invisible world. A tree that had disappeared from the orchanvilly field floated near his window. Then a mygratia flew by him; it squawked as it passed.

Wait a minute! Wasn't that oddity-bot Four-Two who just went by? Wasn't he e-raced? Major Tomm thought.

"E-RACER! ODDITY-BOTS! Come in!" he yelled as he banged his communicator against the steering wheel. "Where is everybody? Where am I?"

CHAPTER EIGHTEEN

KINGPIN

The gang left the fuelsolage garage with no way to understand what had happened to Major Tomm. Instead, they went back to enjoying the outcome of the race. RV had won, and Deluxe was out of harm's way.

Madame Insane reminded them, "You know, we promised Deluxe that we would all meet her back at the DLG after the races. RV, I think you should go ahead. We'll all catch up with you."

Fast Earnie said, "Let's all go … right now!" He was energetic and ready for everyone to see Deluxe immediately.

Madame Insane shook her head, "No, baby. RV needs some time with Deluxe alone."

It took a while, but Fast Earnie finally understood that his wife was encouraging a courtship. "Oh, I get it," he said quietly.

Madame Insane pulled RV aside and whispered to him, "Listen! You go see that girl and tell her how you feel."

RV hesitated. "You know, one time she did kiss me on the cheek out of gratitude."

"See?"

RV continued, "Yeah, but then she told me I looked like a blue bowling pin."

Madame Insane thought, *Here is an incredible athlete with a fine character. He is completely humble and smitten with the girl he loves.* She enjoyed RV's honesty

"Look, RV," she explained, "if you're a bowling pin, then you be her kingpin. Go on, now. Woo that girl and sweep her off her feet."

"Okay," said RV as he hugged her. "Thanks."

He headed out toward the DLG. He wanted to calm down from the excitement of the day, so on his way, he took a stroll in the orchanvilly field. He pulled a small shovel from the compartment in his belly, dug up an orchanvilly, and placed it on a piece of canvas. He carefully wrapped the plant and tied it with a piece of cord so that the flower could be replanted.

When RV arrived at the café, he was a bit nervous. He peaked through the window, held the flower behind his back, and opened the door.

All the girls shouted, "RV's here!"

Deluxe ran up to greet him.

"RV, you won! You even did it with your new wheel. I'm so proud of you. You've won the Major Races! This has to be the most incredible thing that's ever happened to you."

"No," RV said seriously. He became very quiet, and then he continued. "Winning the Major Races wasn't the most incredible thing that's ever happened to me."

He had her full attention.

"It wasn't?" Deluxe asked, puzzled.

"No, Deluxe," said RV as he worked up the courage to reveal his heart to her. "You are. You're the most incredible thing that's ever happened to me." He showed her the orchanvilly and placed it in her hand. Then he leaned over, kissed her lightly on the cheek, and said, "I love you, Deluxe."

She was stunned. She took a deep breath and touched the spot where he had kissed her.

"RV, I love you, too," she said tenderly.

The adrenalin rush that RV experienced from hearing those words was more intense than anything he had ever known. He stood dumbfounded for several seconds. Finally he sighed with relief and smiled from ear to ear. This was unexpected. She loved him!

The café's big screen abruptly sounded off with the harsh distraction of GAS: the Global Alarm System.

"NEWS FLASH!" blared the announcer. "The Zein Press announced today that there is growing concern as to the whereabouts of Major Tomm. He has not been seen since his disappearance earlier today at the Major Races. Experts say that this is most likely one of the Major's planned performances. However, until he is found, all authority over his vast empire will be transferred into the hands of Major Tomm's associate, E-racer. The Zein Press and Eccentric Racing Network will keep you updated on this story."

About the Author

L. M. Ruttkay grew up in the United States of America, where she graduated with a Bachelor of Fine Arts degree from the University of California. She lives in San Diego.